THE STORM IS PASSING OVER

THE STORM IS PASSING OVER

CHARLES R. BUTTS JR.

WILLIAMS & KING PUBLISHERS

ISBN: 978-0-999840665
Printed in the USA

Williams and King Publishers
304 Ocoee Apopka Rd, Ocoee, FL 34761

O courage my soul and let us journey on,

For though the night is dark, it won't be very long.

O thanks be to God, the morning light appears,

And the storm is passing over. Hallelujah, Hallelujah

Hallelujah, the storm is passing over, Hallelujah! "

Charles Albert Tindley 1905

Storms are temporary,

Blessings last forever.

CHAPTER 1

Time never slows or ends. Embracing its passage and changes gifts us with memories, happiness, and grace. Any attempt to manipulate, outrun or turn back its hands only accelerates the storms that are sure to follow.

It passes so rapidly, and there seems to never be enough of it. Winter, I'm wearing it well, if I say so myself. The journey's been incredible, my body's feeling heavier, but my wisdom and focus has never been sharper. I'm eighty years young and proud of every wrinkle and creaky joint. Only Frankie calls me, *Scooter* now. To everyone else around here, I'm known as *Pops, Daddy, Gramps, Grandpa,* and *Poppy*. Away from the farm though, I'm Mr. Flood. Although I reflect on past seasons from time to time, I'm always content in the present. Besides, I'll take winter's wisdom over summer's vitality any day, it's one of the ways I measure progress.

These tired eyes of mine have witnessed a lot of change. But today, they sparkle and shine. Frankie and I will commemorate our fiftieth anniversary by renewing our vows, and of course, all of our children, grandchildren, and great-grandchildren are here to celebrate with us. Everyone's here, except that oldest son of mine and that social climbing wife of his. It's almost time for the ceremony, and he is late, as usual.

Lately, business has been more important to him. I'm just as nervous and excited as I was fifty years ago. She's still my everything, and as beautiful as ever, I can hardly wait to be alone with her tonight. There's nothing wrong with feeling like an eighty-year-old teenager, I suppose. Next to dancing and holding my beloved in my arms tonight, I'm also excited about the special guests who'll be present to celebrate with us. Uncle Clem and the entire gang will be here soon to honor Frankie and me, but more importantly, to formally meet my successor, my beautiful granddaughter Celeste, or *CiCi* for short.

In our rich family history, everyone with the sight has been male, so I was pretty surprised at first to see a female born with a veil. I've been grooming her since birth, and despite the rough patches she experiences with her father from time to time, she's more than ready. *CiCi* is only twenty-five, she has a seven-year-old son and is pregnant with her second. She's married to Porter King, a deputy sheriff with the Hale County Sheriff's Department.

I'm proud to say our name has become an international brand. Flood Industries is now the largest privately owned conglomerate in the world. I'm even prouder to say that, it's the result of our combined efforts: Frankie, myself, our children and even our grandchildren. Over the years, we've added divisions dedicated to hospitals, research and development labs, pharmaceuticals, jet sales/leasing, and entertainment (to include film, television, distribution, music streaming and concert promotion).

Our luxury hotels, resorts and casinos in Las Vegas, Monte Carlo, and Cuba are performing fabulously. The Financial Services Division includes banks, investment firms, and hedge funds. Last but not least, we have a sports and talent agency, a hair care and cosmetic line, and even a professional basketball team.

The NBA Board of Governors just unanimously approved our purchase of the Atlanta Hawks. However, I'm most proud of our non-profit organization: The Flood Foundation. We provide assistance to the third world and developing countries that include digging wells for clean water, housing, medicine, schools, building places of worship, and after-school community centers. We also provide community centers and better schools in inner-city neighborhoods throughout the U.S., concentrating on homelessness and literacy. We give out hundreds of college scholarships yearly and sit on the board of all one hundred and seven HBCUs (Historically Black Colleges and Universities).

There's no doubt life has been good to all of us, and our tree's strong roots and branches now flower and bloom over the entire planet. But enough about that. Money and power to a certain extent are fine, but only when you're its steward opposed to it being yours. We choose to use it as a tool to better the lives of others.

Our quaint little town has undergone some major cosmetic changes as well. Town square remains intact, but the population's boom is a result of the influx of retirees moving back home. This has led to the building of more housing, restaurants, hotels, car dealerships, a movie theater and bowling alley. And, of course, Super Walmart, Target and Home Depot have found us as well.

I've also made some tweaks to our beautiful farm. We made additions to the main house because our grandkids are practically here all the time. We keep the pond stocked with bass, cats and bream just so we can fish them out. We added a full-size gym, complete with an indoor pool and sauna, along with more walking and biking trails for Frankie and me. I expanded the indoor theater and added an amphitheater, for bands and movies outside whenever the weather permits it.

But the most significant changes I made are the ones unseen to most. In addition to adding security for the entire property, I completely changed the trunk of our tree. I left the main rooms intact, but I had all the tunnels leading out to the property walled, paved and lighted.

I also put in a full-sized kitchen, complete with all the appliances, including a freezer and full bar, and totally stocked with food, water, and drinks. I added bedrooms and bathrooms also. I had an elevator installed at the top of the greenhouse. I had a runway and a hangar added on our property as well. Unc used to say, "Cover all your bases and prepare for war during peacetime."

I also added a driving range and a horse farm. We all caught the flying bug years ago, and most of us are licensed pilots. There's an impressive collection of Cesnas, Citations and even a couple of helicopters in our hangar. We also have golf carts to get around the property when we don't feel like walking.

Frankie and I have been retired for some time now, and aside from traveling or sitting in on an occasional board or foundation meeting, we spend every waking and sleeping moment together. There are no words to adequately express what she means to me, our love is boundless. Handheld strolls, sunrises, sunsets, passion and time with our family are priceless blessings. A day hasn't passed without witnessing a spirit coming or going. As I've grown older, my gift has become stronger and crystal clear.

It's almost showtime, and that boy of mine still hasn't arrived yet. I think I'll ask his son Phillip to stand with me. Everything looks as beautiful as it did fifty years ago. Both he and CiCi, love, honor and respect Reese unconditionally; however, he never spends any time with them or his grandson. I think he resents the fact that Celeste got pregnant in high school and is ashamed of his own son because he is a successful artist who shunned following his footsteps and forged his own path.

Other than being a licensed mortician, he wants nothing to do with the family businesses. Blood is blood and family is family. I pray he changes his ways and appreciates that family, and growing those relationships, are far more important than anything else before it's too late.

For whatever reason, pleasing his father-in-law Heinrich and the rest of the so-called bigwigs in business is more important to him than his family. It just breaks Frankie's heart to see him mistreat his children and grandchild. He was raised far better than this. All he's concerned with is money and the trappings that come with it.

He loves being on the cover of business magazines, attending A-list parties and being mentioned in the high society pages of newspapers. Because Phillip is a world-renowned artist, he invites him to events, to show him off. He refuses to attend unless his sister and her family are also invited.

We raised him to listen to and follow his heart, but I'm afraid his ego and that new wife of his, have drowned out his heart's voice. He's headed down a slippery slope and if he's not careful, he'll completely lose himself and sight of what matters most in life: God, love, family and relationships.

The good Lord has blessed my Frankie and me with a reasonable portion of health and strength. He's blessed us far beyond our wildest dreams. But my heart tells me a huge storm has been brewing for some time now, I can just feel it in my bones. Although I feel it's rapidly approaching, I pray it won't come today, or at least, I hope not. Because fifty years ago today, my life changed and has grown more prosperous and stronger every moment since.

Charles R. Butts Jr.

CHAPTER 2

The ceremony was as beautiful and as breathtaking today as it was fifty years ago. Everything was picturesque. The courtyard was adorned with beautiful flowers and candles and framed by a colorful sunset. Beautiful music was playing by an amazing orchestra and was accompanied by our favorite singers. Our dearest family and friends were in attendance, and standing near the rear of the courtyard taking everything in was Uncle Clem and the rest of my family.

Frankie, even three generations deeper, looked so beautiful being escorted to the altar by our other two sons, Clement and David. I don't know if there were more tears than sweat running down my face. My palms were moist and my hands trembled. There was a hint

9

of concern though, when for a second it looked like Frankie stumbled a little halfway down the aisle.

After professing our love before God, family and friends, we sealed our sacred vows once more with a passionate kiss. After more photos, we all assembled in the reception tent for more photos and to cut our cake. We proudly listened as our children, grandchildren and a few close friends toasted our love. It goes without saying, I had a few shots of Uncle Clem's finest whiskey I'd been saving.

After our supper, and with Reese still M.I.A., everyone present was dancing, mingling and enjoying themselves. I kissed Frankie on the cheek and told her I needed to go down to the greenhouse and introduce CiCi to some very important kinfolk. Playfully waving her finger and winking at CiCi, Frankie said, "Okay, but don't be too long. You promised me some dancing, and we have a long, long night of romance ahead of us."

CiCi smiled, grabbed Frankie's hand and said, "Oooh, you go, Gram! In that case, we'll hurry right back!"

Outside, the moon was full and the stars were bright. On the drive over, Cici could hardly contain her excitement. She's waited patiently for this special moment. When the elevator opened up at the bottom, they were all there waiting, enveloped in incredibly bright light. Uncle Clem smiled and said, "Hey son, long time no see! Aren't you a sight for perfect eyes, and who is this beautiful young lady with you?"

"Hey, Unc! Hello everyone! I'm pleased to introduce my granddaughter and successor, Mrs. Celeste Flood King."

Their smiles made the room appear even brighter. Great-grandma could hardly contain her glee. "Come here, baby, let us get a good look at you. You're so beautiful, and we have a lot in common. I became pregnant with Clement when I was around your age, and my folks shunned and sent me away. Keep loving your Daddy anyhow, he'll come around sooner or later. You have a fine man, a beautiful child and another one coming. I see a lot of me and my ways in you, and if you're not the spitting image of your great-great-great grandma, I'll eat my hat."

"Thank you, ma'am. Gramps and Gram have been wonderful to us. I may be a King by marriage, but Flood blood courses through my veins."

"Amen to that, young lady!" chimed great-great Grandpa Buck. We know you're going to take us to even higher heights. Always remember, that between the Lord Almighty and us, you'll never be alone."

Turning towards me, he smiled and said, "Son, we're all are just blown away with what you've done with the business! And I mean every Flood when I say that!"

"Thank you, sir, but I can't take all the credit for that. This is the result of three generations of Floods putting their heads and hearts together for a common cause. It's what we've always done, and what we'll continue to do."

"That's sweet music to our ears, young lady.!"

"Thanks, sir!" Mama and Pop stepped forward and said, "Congratulations to you and Frankie for fifty wonderful years together. You've made your father and me so very proud."

"Indeed we are son, though we're not surprised. We've always known what you're capable of and are proud of all you've done."

"Thank you both, you mean everything to me."

"You're so very welcome. It sure is an honor to formally meet you CiCi! We've watched you since birth, and you're definitely a Flood through and through."

"Thanks so very much great-grandma! I'm honored to meet you and great-grandpa as well."

Uncle Clem smiled at CiCi and said, "Baby girl, do you mind getting a little more acquainted with your kinfolks, while I step over here and bend your Grandpa's ear for a bit. We'll be back directly, okay?"

"Yes, sir, that'll be just fine." Standing near one of the stills, I reached on the shelf, grabbed a jar, screwed off the lid and inhaled the bouquet before taking a hearty gulp.

"Mmmnn, I see you've built up quite a tolerance for the recipe. Good, huh?"

"Yes, Sir, I've acquired a taste through the years, though I try to indulge myself on special occasions only. I'll admit that's not always the case though. What's on your mind? I feel there's something else you want to talk about. I can practically hear your wheels turning."

"No, other than to tell you again how proud we all are of all of you. Winter sure does look good on you, both of you as a matter of fact. Despite your mountaintops, being covered with snow, the fire in your eyes and hearts still burns bright."

"Thanks, I've always followed my heart and tried to keep my promise to the best of my ability. I've had some very huge shoes to fill."

"I wouldn't say that, but you have indeed son, and then some. We love what you've done to the home place too, especially down here in the trunk. I love this elevator, I wish I'd thought of it."

"It was built out of necessity Unc. It got to the point that these old, arthritic knees couldn't take climbing up and down the stairs any longer. All that running and jumping finally caught up with me, I guess. I definitely had one put in the both the main and guest houses too. All is well, except that oldest boy of mine. It's always business first and family last with him. I've never seen anything like it. Was Dad like this?"

"They're very similar, though he's far more driven than Buddy ever was. Maybe ten times more even. Keep the faith son, time and circumstances both have a way of humbling folks, and showing them what matters most in life."

"Is there something you're not telling me?"

"I'm not talking about anything or anyone, just talking about what I'm talking about. Besides, you know life doesn't work like that. Even if I wanted to tell you anything, I wouldn't. Your choices determine the future. Everyone writes and creates their own story, staying in the present moment with that huge heart and gift of yours is what has brought you and Frankie here fifty years later. Never ignore the present's truth for the future's mysteries."

"You're right as usual. Speaking of Frankie, we'd best be getting back before she comes after me. She's as feisty as ever-maybe even feistier."

"Okay, we won't hold y'all any longer. We just wanted to congratulate you and formally meet our next leader." Turning to CiCi, Uncle Clem continued, "Young lady, we're so very proud to officially meet you. We know you're gonna guide our family even farther. We decided to wait until you were an adult before formally meeting you. Just as we were here for your Grandpa, we'll always be here for you, too."

"Thank you all for your kindness, love, and faith in me. I promise my best always, and to never let you guys down," CiCi said.

"Bye everybody!" I said.

"Bye, you two!" Everyone smiled and waved before walking through the wall and out of sight.

Charles R. Butts Jr.

CHAPTER 3

O h my God, Gramps! I can't believe what just happened. Meeting our ancestors was amazing! When my time comes, I promise to always do my very best," CiCi said.

"We know you will, Baby Girl. There's no one on this side of the sun more qualified than you. Always stay connected and reach out to them from time to time, they're always eager to assist us. You'll never have to worry about going it alone, I never did nor did any of our predecessors."

"I promise I will Gramps! I trust my heart, and all of you as well."

"That's great to hear because neither will they ever deceive you."

The band's music grew louder as we approached the tent. Inside, Reese and Greta had finally arrived, along with his in-laws Heinrich and Ingrid Klaus. Once inside, Reese made a beeline towards me. "Hey, Pop! Happy fiftieth anniversary to you and Mom!"

"Thank you, son. What took you so long to get here? You promised you'd be here yesterday at the latest. I chose Phillip to stand with me in your stead."

"I know, and I'm so very sorry for that. But I have some very exciting news that will more than make up for it."

"If your news has anything to do with business, it'll have to keep until me and your mother return from our trip." I should have known he'd show up pitching something that I'd surely oppose. Besides, there's something not right about Heinrich. I've always had a strange feeling about him, but I can't seem to put my finger on what it is. He just doesn't appear genuine to me, at least not yet anyway.

"It can't wait that long, Pop, please just give me fifteen minutes of your time to make my presentation. That's all I ask."

"Sorry son, down here family takes precedence over everything. In case you'd forgotten, this is a celebration for your mother and I renewing our vows. Our fiftieth anniversary is far more important than any perspective deal you've brought here to us. Now, where's your Mother, brothers, and sisters?"

"They've gone to the house and are waiting for us. We just need to meet long enough to vote, and I'll get out of you and Mom's way."

Frankie and the kids were all in the conference room waiting. The solemn looks on their faces all but confirmed my suspicions. Reese began: "Ok since everyone's here, let's begin. Pop, an opportunity to acquire controlling interest in AQR is now available, but since we only have a short window to make the deal, let me lay out the plan. I've petitioned the SEC to make Flood Industries a publicly traded company. The billions we'll earn from the IPO will be more than enough to purchase the remaining blocks of stock to acquire AQR and bring it under the Flood umbrella. Heinrich is already on board with this plan, and all I need is a majority approval to move forward on this. Let's take a vote, shall we?"

When everyone's eyes trained on me, I said, "I don't think we need to vote, son, because your mother and I are voting *no*. It's too risky, and it's not what we Floods are about. Heinrich, didn't you lose control of your family's company when you took it public? Didn't your new board of directors vote to remove you as CEO?"

Looking stunned, Heinrich dropped his head and said, "Yes, it's true, I was removed. I lost control of a company that my great-grandfather started from nothing, for the lure of more money and power. I lost my heart while lusting and chasing my ego's desires. It's something I'll regret forever, and it's unnecessary for all of you to take the same risk."

"I appreciate you saying that sir, but even if you hadn't, my answer would still be *no*. Flood Industries is the result of generations of hard work and sacrifice. There will never be a chance of it being run by anyone other than a Flood. I swore an oath promising that it would never be. I'm sorry son, but I and your mother vote *no*."

The other children nodded, looked at their brother and voted *nay*. Incensed, Reese stood, slammed his fist on the table and screamed, "Don't you people understand what we're passing up! We can have it all!"

I stood up and calmly said, "We clearly understand son, but what saddens me is you seem to have forgotten that we will always remain a private, family-owned and controlled entity. We already have it all. Balance sheets and profit margins don't define or drive us. We're stewards of a fortune the next fifty or so of Floods couldn't even begin to spend. We also feel obligated for the continued happiness and continuity of all of our employees and everyone our foundation assists. Now calm down and let's go out there and celebrate. Our guests have waited for us long enough."

"I'm in no mood to celebrate, I'm going home, although I truly respect and admire the love you and Mom share. It's true the risks are minimal, but I had all the bases covered."

Frankie stood, walked over to him, hugged him and said, "Please stay a while son, we haven't seen you and Greta in so long, plus I know CiCi, Phillip, Porter and the baby would love to spend some time with you."

"Sorry, Mom, I gotta get back to Atlanta. Got early morning meetings, plus the Governor's ball is tomorrow evening."

"Well, can you at least dance with your dear old Mom once."

"Sure Mom, how can I ever refuse you anything." Looking at his siblings and me, he said, "Someday you guys will learn to trust me."

Grabbing and shaking his hand, I said, "Son, we all trust and appreciate your hard work. But this is about keeping a promise to your Uncle Clem, as well as every Flood that has come before you. I hope you'll understand that someday."

"Let's just agree to disagree, Pop."

"Ok, son, but no hard feelings, right?"

When I tried to hug him, he pulled away and said, "Sorry, Pop, it's going to take some time for me to digest this."

Clement stepped toward Reese, shoved him and said, "Don't you ever disrespect our father!"

David separated them and said, "We're not doing this today, and especially not now. This is Mom and Pop's moment. You owe both of them your respect and an apology."

"I don't apologize for anything I've said or done tonight. Mama, I am going to have to take a raincheck on that dance, I'm leaving."

With tears streaming down Frankie's face, she said, "Please don't go Reese, please." Trying to stand, she collapsed and fell to the floor. Lying there unconscious and unresponsive, we all looked at each other and feared the worst.

CHAPTER 4

Amid the shock and panic, the boys rushed their mother to Reese's helicopter on the lawn. We airlifted Frankie to Druid City Memorial in Tuscaloosa.

On the flight over, Beverly attended to Frankie and I held her hand and prayed as hard as I could. The medical staff was waiting for us on the helipad when we landed and rushed Frankie in. She had a pulse but wasn't conscious.

I sat in the waiting room looking around, trying to sense and see if any of our people had come for her. Seeing no one here slowed my heart down a bit, but I witnessed more than a few people dropping their suits, reuniting and following the kin that had come for them. Aside from Frankie stumbling earlier, I hadn't felt or seen any signs of anything being wrong or her becoming ill.

About forty-five minutes later, Beverly came out from the back with some forms. That and the solemn face and her tears told me something was seriously wrong.

"What is it, Baby Girl, how's your Mom, and what's that you've brought with you."

"I'm sorry, Daddy, it appears Mommy suffered a massive stroke. There's considerable hemorrhaging around her brain, and we feel immediate surgery is her only option. I need you to sign these forms authorizing the staff to begin prepping her for surgery."

I took the form from her and scribbled my signature on it. "Will you be assisting?"

"No, Daddy, when family's involved, it's not wise to participate."

"Ok, I understand. Can I see her for a minute before they take her?"

Kissing me on the cheek and squeezing me with a hug I so desperately needed, she said, "Of course. I'll go to the waiting area and bring everyone up to speed. They should all be here now."

"Ok, thanks."

Inside Frankie's room, I slid a chair beside the bed and took her hand in mine. Interlocking our fingers, I kissed her hand and told her how much I loved her. Just seeing her like this, hooked up to all those monitors, pierced my heart down to the depths of my soul.

I leaned closer and said, "I'm here, Sweetie, and I'm not going anywhere. You're my everything, I love you so much. You healed and helped me find my heart so long ago, and have continuously showered me with a love I didn't even know was possible. I'm so grateful and forever indebted to you for our children, grandchildren and great-grandchildren."

Bright light filled the room, then Uncle Doc and Frankie's mom Beverly entered the room behind it.

"Hey son," Uncle Doc said.

"Uncle Doc, is that you? I almost didn't recognize you. How's it going?"

Chuckling, he said, "It's ok, son, we haven't seen each other in a long time. Besides, other than a few old, grainy photographs, you never really saw much of my younger version. I can't begin to explain how wonderful it's going. I want you to meet someone though I'm sure you already know who this is."

"You're Ms. Beverly, right?"

"Yes, I am. But first, let me thank you for loving and caring for my child so very much."

"Believe me, ma'am, the pleasure is all mine. I'm hoping and praying I'll be allowed to continue doing so. Are you here to take her from me?"

"That depends on the two of you."

"What do you mean?"

"It's entirely her choice, and she'll probably want to stay here a little longer with you." Beverly smiled, "Let love guide you both like it always has. It always helps us make our best decisions."

"Love and prayer, ma'am. What God has for us is for us. Always has been and always will be."

"As it should be," said Doc. "We're all so very proud of everything the two of you accomplished."

"Thanks, Uncle Doc, but it wasn't Frankie and me alone that's built this. Our kids and grandkids are major contributors to our brand. And of course, we always follow God."

"Can never go wrong doing that, son. Well, we're going to take our leave now, but we'll be around if you need us."

"Ok, it's so good seeing you Uncle Doc, and nice meeting you ma'am."

"The pleasure is all mine."

They vanished, just before the orderlies entered and wheeled Frankie to surgery. Everyone was already in the waiting area when I got there. I saw fear and concern on every face present. Reese was sobbing uncontrollably. He stood up and hugged me tightly.

"I'm so very sorry, Pop, this is all my fault. My behavior was totally uncalled for. I upset Mom and caused her collapse. All she wanted was for me to stay a little longer and spend some time with all of you."

"It's not your fault son. Your Mom's stroke probably would have happened regardless. I suspect she's been hiding how she was truly feeling for some time now."

Bella hugged me and said, "Do you need us to do anything, Daddy?"

"No baby girl, just need all of you to keep the faith and pray as hard as you possibly can. I think I'll go downstairs to the chapel and do the same. I need to be alone."

"Ok, Daddy, we'll keep you posted. We'll be up here praying as well.

Charles R. Butts Jr.

CHAPTER 5

In the chapel, I lit a candle and sat on the front pew. Burying my face into my hands, I prayed to God in silence. I'm so very grateful for these past fifty years and all of the blessings, trials and memories that have come with it.

Hospitals are always difficult for me to get focused and quiet all of the internal noise because they're usually filled with spirits. Spirits coming here to gather with family and spirits leaving to join them. When I removed my hands, Frankie stood in front of me. She wasn't shrouded in bright light, and her silver cord showed me she was still tethered to her body.

Smiling beautifully, she sat beside me and said, "This has been some fiftieth-anniversary celebration, hasn't it? The day definitely didn't go like I planned. I wanted it to be special, and marry you in the sight of God, and with the entire family present one last time. I haven't been well for some time, and I'm so very sorry I hid it from you. Obviously, I didn't do too great of a job doing that either. Truth is, I've known for a while that the time has come for me to cross that river. I just wanted to create one last beautiful memory to take with me. There are no words to describe how much I'm going to miss you. I hope and pray you can forgive me."

"Baby, there's nothing to forgive, in fact I need to thank you. You've blessed me so much with your love and made me so very happy. We've had a wonderful journey together. Five children, twenty-one grandchildren and almost seven great-grandchildren later. Not to mention increasing the family's fortune - a hundredfold together. If I never receive another blessing from God, and if He never answers another prayer from me, He's done more than enough - more than I could have ever imagined or hoped for. I was a mess when I first came home, and your patience and love transformed me and made me want to love again and be worthy of being loved. You're solely responsible for that. Some people live their entire lives never even coming close to experiencing the kind of love and companionship God blessed me with when He made us one: one heartbeat and one soul. Whatever sadness and loneliness that's sure to come will be minimal, compared to our fifty years of joy and happiness. Of course, I'll miss you terribly, but I will tuck you and all of our incredible memories inside my heart forever. I'll keep counsel with CiCi, and will continue leading our family until our forever begins."

Teary-eyed Frankie said, "I feel the same way sweetheart, we've been so blessed. Sorry we never got our first dance."

"It's ok, we will someday."

"We'd better because I'm going to hold you to that. What's happened to Reese? His behavior is disturbing, to say the least. It's one thing to be ambitious, but I hardly recognize him anymore. He appears to have gone mad with power. I miss the sweet, caring son who once put God and family above the treasure, adulation and fame."

"I know, I suppose fame's glory can be addictive to some and it appears his ego has nearly swallowed his heart and spirit whole. What troubles me the most is how he treats CiCi, Phillip and the baby. He ignores them but bends over backward for that new wife of his and her folks. Don't worry, he'll eventually find his way someday. Sometimes, you have to hit rock bottom before you remember who you really are and what's most important in your life. More often than not, his fall will shake him to his core and hopefully bring the real Reese back."

"I have no doubt it'll do just that."

"Neither do I."

"I suppose I should be going, I'll be out of surgery soon. I need a favor."

"Anything, sweetheart, you just name it."

"My body is going to be placed on a ventilator, so I'll need you to be strong for me and allow them to disconnect it, but let everyone say their goodbyes. Do that for me?"

With tears streaming from my eyes, I smiled and said, "You know I can't refuse you anything."

"Ok, thanks dear heart. I know it's not an easy thing for me to ask you. Oh, one more thing, I won't ever come around to see you. I know our people visit you from time to time, but I won't ever do that. That would be too hard for me to do, probably for you as well I imagine. The next time you see me, it'll be time for us to begin our forever. It'll be time to dance. I love you with all of my heart, and thanks so much for this wonderful journey."

"You're very welcome, but believe me, the pleasure was and will forever be all mine. Our love is forever."

"Forever love, indeed." I left the chapel without looking back, got on the elevator and rejoined the rest of the family.

Charles R. Butts Jr.

CHAPTER 6

By now, the rest of the family had arrived. The sad faces and tears made me know they 've just been told about Frankie's prognosis.

Beverly only confirmed what her mom told me earlier: The hemorrhaging was far worse than the surgeons had anticipated, and the damage was irreversible. A ventilator was keeping her alive and my permission was needed to remove her from it. I assembled everyone and relayed Frankie's wishes.

With a saddened heart, when everyone was saying their goodbyes, I stepped out of the room and signed the consent forms, authorizing the doctors to disconnect the machine. After calling ahead to the parlor to send a hearse for Frankie's body, Porter and CiCi drove me back to the farm.

Back at the farm, preparations for Frankie's home going celebration began in earnest. Even though our family hasn't experienced a loss since Grammy all those years ago, the same protocol that every Flood has received would be strictly adhered to. Beverly and Bella insisted on preparing their mother's body, and CiCi asked to help with her hair, nails, and makeup. Fortunately, my only responsibility was greeting and mingling with the many guests that are sure to come.

Over the next four days, my kids and grandkids made me so proud. The genuine love, care, respect and support they showed everyone and each other warmed my heart. Our friends and family loved on and comforted each other.

Frankie's home going celebration took place on a warm and sunny July day. Beautiful flowers and moving tributes enveloped the farm in love. Burying your beloved of fifty years, only days after renewing your vows, felt weird to say the least and of course, at the cemetery, I acknowledged our ancestors who were present.

The usual celebratory festivities took place afterward, and a few days later, everyone departed for their homes. The kids offered to stay with me a while, but I insisted they get back to their lives. It was important to me to try and restore some normalcy.

We have a company and a foundation to maintain, and a lot of people depend on us. Even still the world feels a whole lot different and so empty and lonely to me without Frankie. Deep in my heart, she'll always remain, because someday I know we'll be together again.

A couple of days later, I was under the greenhouse recording Frankie's passing in the family Bible and placing her obituary inside of it, when Uncle Clem appeared.

"How's my favorite nephew?"

"I'm trying to hang in there Unc, I'm actually a lot better than I thought I'd be. I can truly say I understand how you felt when you lost Aunt Lizzy."

"I'm happy to hear that son but truth be told, I don't know if all of the sadness completely leaves us. It's all those wonderful memories that keep us keeping on. Time never helps us get over our losses, but it'll definitely help you get through it. That, and knowing in your heart where she is, and someday you'll see her again. The reunion will be amazing, just trust me."

"I always have, and I always will."

"Good, because she misses you just as much, if not more."

"Thanks, Unc. You always know how to make me feel better."

"You're always welcome, son."

As he was tucking the obituary away in his coat pocket, my phone rang.

"Hello."

"Hey, Pops, this is Clement."

"Hey son, how's it going? What's on your mind?"

"We have a problem. The SEC just contacted me and wanted me to confirm the IPO that's just been filed. They said they received the final documents from us two days ago, and we're scheduled to be in New York next Monday. Even after we voted it down, Reese is trying to go ahead and push it through anyway."

"What did you tell them?"

"I told him the rest of the shareholders voted against it, then asked them what they needed from us to negate the filing. I was told they only need a certified affidavit with the signatures of the majority opposing it."

"Ok, here's what I need you to do. Get the affidavit signed by everyone and submit it. Cut off Reese's access to all company monies, run a report on all of his financials and tell your sisters and brothers we need to convene to discuss it and him. Got it?"

"Yes, sir, I'm on it, Pops. What do you want me to tell Reese?"

"Tell him his presence is mandatory. I'll deal with him when he gets here."

"Will do, Pops. I'll call you after I take care of everything."

"Ok son. Thanks." Turning to Uncle Clem I said, "That boy! I'm just dumbfounded that he still has the gall to attempt to deceive us, even after we unanimously vetoed it. With everything that's happened since then, I'll make my intentions crystal clear to him."

"If it means anything, you have our complete support. You have never led us wrong. Well, I'll leave you to it. Catch you later."

"Ok Unc. Thanks again. I look forward to it." He left and I grabbed a couple of jars of whiskey before heading to the house. I was so angry, I felt a little dizzy.

Charles R. Butts Jr.

CHAPTER 7

I was pacing back and forth in the conference room with David and Clement. We were waiting for Reese to arrive so the meeting could commence. Bella was with her family in Italy, and Beverly was attending a conference in California. They called in to cast their votes.

About forty-five minutes later, Reese strode into the conference room. Surprisingly, he was smiling and whistling like he didn't have a care in the world. After exchanging pleasantries with everyone, he took his seat, smiled and asked if he could make a statement before we began. "Look, everyone, I know what I did was wrong, and I know why we're here. I'm not here to argue or be hostile. Pop, I'm going to make it easy and less awkward for everyone present.

While I don't believe I was wrong for trying to go ahead with the IPO, and would probably do the same thing again if given the chance, I'm here to offer an apology anyhow and submit my resignation."

"Son, I think I speak for everyone present when I say we accept both your apology and your resignation. I'm so glad we handled this professionally, and that it didn't have to get hostile."

"Ok, Pop, since that's settled, I just want to say one more thing before I leave."

"Sure thing, son, you have the floor. What is it?"

"Well, I was thinking, since I'm no longer a part of Flood Industries, I'd be open to selling back my ten percent share. I have a deal or two on my plate and could definitely use the extra capital. What do you guys say?"

"Well, son, I don't have a problem with that. It's never happened before in our family's history, but since you've wisely resigned, it's fine with me if it's fine with your sisters and brothers."

After everyone agreed, I instructed Clement to cut Reese a check for his ten percent. We also had him sign an agreement divesting himself forever from Flood Industries. He'll need a majority vote to ever return. Clement was appointed to handle the day to day, and Bella, Beverly and David agreed to not only take on more responsibilities for themselves, but we thought it's the perfect time to delegate more tasks to my grandchildren.

Reese said his goodbyes to his siblings and vowed to stay in touch with them. When he made it to the helicopter, he turned, hugged me and said, "I'm sorry Pop, so sorry that it came to all of this."

"Like I said earlier, we forgive you and we will always love you. You'll always be a Flood, and this will always be your home - you can come back anytime. I hope everything works out for you, you know I'm your biggest fan. Make your mom and me proud."

"Thanks, Pop, I'll do my very best. I'll send the helicopter back when I get home."

"That's ok, I insist you keep it. Stay in touch son, and know I'll always be here for you. We all will."

"That's great to know Pop. Thanks again, and I'll touch bases with you real soon. Bye for now."

"Why don't you stay for supper, I'm sure CiCi and Phillip would love to see you."

"Can I get a raincheck? I'm a little pushed for time, and I need to get back to Atlanta to put the finishing touches on a deal I have pending. I'll give them a call and set up something for later though, I promise."

"Ok, safe travels son."

"See you, Pop, and thanks again."

I stood on the helipad and watched the helicopter until it was out of sight, then took a cart back to the main house. I couldn't tell if I was more relieved or saddened. It feels like a mighty bolt of lightning has struck our tree and damaged one of its branches.

CHAPTER 8

Time passes whether we want it to or not, and I learned a long time ago to move right along with it. It brought normalcy and rhythm back to the farm. It kept life marching forward, and with summer coming to an end, I missed Frankie more and more every day.

Time can't erase or heal grief, but it does make it bearable. Granted, I've accepted her passing, but a part of me left with her. I occupy my days with checkers, chess, reading and being run ragged by that great-grandson of mine, Sterling. If I could just bottle and sell a little of his energy, it could corner the market.

Reese became the talk of the business world. After gathering some investors, he successfully took over AQR. He was unanimously voted CEO, and the stock continues to soar to record highs. I've yet to see him on TV, in a magazine or on a red carpet not wearing a grin from one ear to the other.

We're all so very proud of him, but I suppose all of those stockholders lining their pockets with the dividends he's earning for them are even prouder. Surprisingly, there's been no conflict between their business and ours. What really pleases me the most is he's also making more of an effort to spend time with his kids and grandchild. He's even building a relationship with his son-in-law. Even without Frankie, I still manage to appreciate all of life's beauty around me. Gorgeous sunrises and sunsets never get old - I enjoy each one more than the last.

I love watching the way Porter and CiCi love on each other. Their love makes me reminisce about Frankie and me the most. Maybe it's because I'm always around them. But truth be told, all of my kids, grandkids and their spouses share the same kind of love and respect for each other. That's what always mattered most to Frankie and me. We pray it's our enduring legacy.

David and his family have been trying to get me to fly up for a visit. I know he's eager to show me the basketball operations and all the plans and projections he and his kids have for it. But I believe these dark storm clouds, swirling winds, and aching joints tell me that trip's going to have to wait for a spell. The forecast calls for severe thunderstorms. The sudden bursts of wind and angry, low hanging dark clouds overhead confirms it.

However, those same clouds appear to hold something a bit more sinister than a mere thunderstorm. Trouble is coming. Trouble with a capital "T"!

Back at the main house, I gathered everyone, and we quickly made our way under the greenhouse. Tornadoes have already touched down in Birmingham and are rapidly headed this way. Tuscaloosa's scheduled to be hit in fifteen or twenty minutes. There's some anxiety here, but there's no need to be. We have everything we need; food, water, supplies, and the generators are all fueled and ready.

The winds are violently picking up and there's a whole lot of noise out there. We clearly hear violent smashing and bumping above us. Even the ground appears to be shaking. I hope everyone here, and in the affected areas have taken cover and are prepared to ride this mighty storm out.

I tried to ease the tension by lightening the mood a bit. I said, "Back in the day, when a storm was coming, Grammy would say, 'Let's just be still and let God do his work.' She didn't even want a phone or TV on. 'Storms will come, but they never last. It's bound to pass over, and it always does. The Lord never brings us to something without taking us through it, and it always leaves us stronger and better than we were before." Everyone's still on edge and I don't believe any of us will sleep much tonight. The wind is roaring like a locomotive's engine.

CHAPTER 9

The following morning, after eating and listening to the news reports, we decided to leave the greenhouse and go outside to survey the damage.

A blue sky, sunshine, and unbelievable devastation greeted us. The entire farm was destroyed, it was a total loss. From the looks of it, those powerful winds uprooted, snapped, and tossed trees around like twigs. The vehicles had been moved and some of them were even turned upside down. The trees that still stood had branches full of debris.

We soon learned that most of Tuscaloosa, Greensboro, and Sawyerville was destroyed; many people were injured and still trapped in homes that had been reduced to rubble. More than a few people perished. It was a chaotic scene. Destruction as far as the eye can see. Even the town's square was ruined.

What's most important right now besides organizing a massive rescue effort, was securing shelter for everyone who'd been displaced, including our family. The Governor declared a state of emergency. Much was lost was in the storm's wake, but it has passed over. It's brought everyone closer and even more determined to rebuild an even stronger community.

Once the rebuilding of the farm began, CiCi's family moved to our place in Tuscaloosa and I moved to Atlanta to live with David's family while the farm was being rebuilt.

Fortunately, neither the family cemetery or greenhouse was damaged, so I still frequented them regularly. Of course, I always made myself available to CiCi. However, by now, there really wasn't anything left to teach her, she was more than ready. I was more concerned about her having a smooth pregnancy because more of our blood was on the way. A child from one of her children will someday succeed her. The responsibility of preparing him or her will rest solely on her shoulders. The past threat of Reese taking our company public and losing control of it has made me take permanent measures to close that loophole.

I'll add a codicil to my will, stipulating the company must forever remain owned by Floods for in-perpetuity. It'll also decree that my shares be bequeathed to CiCi, then passed down through the generations to whoever possesses the gift of sight.

I'm grateful that incident took place because who knows what could have happened if I was no longer on this side. Fortunately, my other kids believe it's in everyone's best interests that Flood Industries forever remain a privately owned entity.

Picturesque sunrises and sunsets are everywhere and are the same up here in Atlanta. I made it my business to enjoy each and every one of them. I also enjoyed taking in some of the basketball games. I'm so very proud of David, and equally proud of all of my kids, really. He and his family never cease to amaze me.

He's a great businessman, but an even greater husband and father. The entire organization is thriving, but what's even greater than that is the Sunday suppers he and Monica have with their kids and grands. I found myself really looking forward to those.

As much as I'm enjoying Atlanta, there's no place like home. Not the home and structures per se, but the land; the sacred ground of my ancestors, land cultivated by and stained with the blood and sweat of generations of Floods.

Everything's restored, but even more important than that,

CiCi's due to give birth any day now. I've had enough city living, and I'm looking forward to getting back to the slow pace of home. There's no place in the whole, wide world like Greensboro, Alabama.

CHAPTER 10

I never imagined it was possible, but the entire home place was now even grander. Of course, there were a few things that couldnever be replaced, but I supposed that's to be expected. Truth be told, I haven't felt my best lately, but my spirits are at an all-time high.

This is a wonderful time because CiCi is in labor, and even though he'll be a King by birth, Flood blood will course through his veins as well. Every birth adds a new branch to our tree, and each branch is special. But this one is extremely special because through this child, CiCi's successor will possibly come to be.

Uncle Clem brought with him a coterie of our ancestors to witness the arrival, bless and give thanks to God for the child. But true to her word, Frankie wasn't one of them. I miss her so much, and Unc assures me that she misses me just the same, if not more. I try to put on a brave face, smile and hide my loneliness and failing health from them, and as usual, they pretend not to notice. No one's fooling anyone, as far as that goes.

After the ancestors extended their congratulations to CiCi and covered her and the baby in prayer, they said their goodbyes. I took a cart over to the cemetery to put fresh flowers on Frankie's grave. It always took away some of the loneliness and sadness. I turned around and saw Uncle Clem standing there. I nodded for him to join me on the bench.

Smiling, he said, "Coming here always made me feel better too. It sure was a wonderful blessing to witness more of our blood coming into the world. Especially, this special one. Someday, he might bring about the next one. How are you holding up, son? You've done an incredible job. You've taken the company to new heights, held the family together and even got that oldest boy of yours to spend more time with his family. You've weathered the passing storm, and rebuilt this place better and stronger than ever."

"I've only tried to keep this family moving forward, Unc. I've given it my all, my very best, every moment of every day."

"We're all so very proud."

"Thanks, Unc, don't know how much longer I can steer this ship. Haven't felt my best lately. It's hard to hold on while missing Frankie so much. My heart aches for her, Unc."

"I know son, just keep giving your best effort while trusting your heart. Storms come, but they always pass. Not all storms are weather related. They're different types, but one constant is that when they come, they're all sure to pass."

"Are you saying more storms are coming?"

"Can't say for sure, son. Like I said, they're all kinds of storms. But we all believe in you and are more than sure you have what it takes to ride them out."

"Thanks for the pep talk, Unc. You always know when I need a word of encouragement. You always know what to say without giving anything away."

"You're always welcome. Your heart knows you're writing your own story and charting your own path. See you around."

"Ok Unc. I look forward to it. See ya."

Charles R. Butts Jr.

CHAPTER 11

The following spring, the entire clan came home for PJ's
christening. It always warms my heart when our whole family
gathers together. I know I'm fading and the finish line is in sight, plus
it's becoming more difficult to hide it. Judging by all the concerned
looks I'm getting from my kids and grandkids, I'm failing miserably
at it.

Everyone was already at church for the ceremony when Reese
saunters in fashionably late. He looks like he hasn't been doing well.
He's lost some weight, and his face sunken and gaunt. Almost looks
like a shell of himself. Looks like I'm not the only one giving the
family cause for concern. His visits have become more sporadic of

late. AQR is in a tailspin. Clement tells me their stock is at an all-time low.

Because of the bear market, a complete crash is imminent. Well structured companies like ours position themselves to profit in both bull and bear markets.

Unknown to him, some time ago, Clement and David formed a shell company, and we have practically purchased all of the available shares; more than enough to force a takeover and wrest control away from the board.

I'm sure his father-in-law used him just to get his hands on our company. I have no doubt he's doing the same thing now. I look forward to informing him that AQR will soon be another Flood Industries acquisition. We neither start or run from wars, but we sure know how to strategically end them.

After supper, Reese, David, Clement and myself were sitting around the fire pit in the courtyard enjoying some whiskey and cigars. Reese seemed really troubled, his hands were trembling.

"So, how are things going at AQR son?" I asked. "We've been noticing that the shares are at an all-time low."

"I feel like I'm fighting two battles, Pop," Reese replied. "Keeping the stock from plummeting any lower and maintaining my position as CEO. Not to mention losing nearly all of my personal fortune. Between my investments and divorcing Greta, I'm mortgaged to the hilt. I could do no wrong and was everyone's friend when profits were soaring and the company was thriving. Now I'm being blamed for everything, even the market crashing is my fault too. The board has called an emergency meeting and I know it is to call for my ouster. I've practically lost everything and I can't seem to come up with a solution. I've failed again."

David walked over to Reese, put his arm around him and said, " Look, you're not a failure, brother, you're a Flood. Someone I love and respect a great deal once told me that in life, storms come, but they don't last forever."

Clement also walked over to Reese and said, "That's right, brother, you know who we are and whose we are, it's always darkest before the dawn. But with our family, it's never over. Our ancestors have overcome far greater challenges than this. We're coming with you to that meeting as a show of unity. Like David says, the game's never over until the final buzzer sounds."

"That's right, son, I think I'll come along too. Got a few choice words for Heinrich, and I want to be looking directly into his eyes when I say them."

Tears streamed down Reese's face as he stood, embraced us all and apologized, "I'm so sorry for everything. I lost my way and allowed my ego to get the best of me again. Nothing's more important than family. I don't even care if I'm fired. I'm done with the business world. I just want to come home if it's ok with you, Pop?"

"Of course it is, it's your home," I replied. "You're always welcome. Nothing would make me happier. Now enough about business. Can an old man enjoy some whiskey and a cigar under these beautiful stars with his three strong sons?" Smiling, they all nodded yes in unison.

CHAPTER 12

The energy in AQR's boardroom shifted drastically when David, Clement and I walked in with Reese. I think our presence startled everyone, especially Heinrich. After exchanging pleasantries, the board's chairman gaveled the meeting to order. Reese nodded to him and he said, "I believe Mr. Klaus has requested the floor first. Sir, if you will."

"Thank you, Mr. Chairman," Mr. Klaus said. "First off, I think I speak for everyone present when I say we're so very honored to have the Floods join us today. Especially you, Mr. Flood. Your reputation precedes itself. As we are all aware, the company is in tatters and sinking fast. The shares are at an all time low. So as much as it pains me to say this, I move for a vote to remove Reese Flood as CEO. Those in favor, say aye, those opposed say nay."

Going around the table, everyone voted "aye", and only Reese voted "nay".

Feigning concern, Mr. Klaus said, "I'm so sorry, Reese, looks like the "ayes" have it. In addition, I further move to appoint myself as CEO. Shall we vote?"

Looking at Reese, Mr. Klaus said, "Sorry, again it's a business decision. It's not personal; you know I still love you like a son. I always will."

Reese nodded, and I stood, looked around the room and said, "Excuse me, Mr. Chairman, may I speak on my son's behalf?"

"Absolutely, Mr. Flood, I think I speak for everyone when I say it's an honor just to have you in our presence."

Heinrich looking puzzled, stood up and said, "I'm happy to see you again, but is this necessary?"

"It's indeed necessary, otherwise I wouldn't have flown all the way up here with my boys."

"Then, by all means, the floor is yours, don't keep us in suspense."

"Well, for starters, yesterday we informed the board that we now own more shares of AQR than anyone. When the stock began to plummet, we bought as much stock as was available; which now means Flood Industries controls AQR. I assured the board that we'd like them to remain and continue to run the day to day on a couple of conditions."

Looking as pale as a ghost, he asked, "What conditions?"

"I thought you'd never ask. First, cut my son a check for his initial investment plus twenty percent, and secondly, fire you with cause and agree to never allow you to darken the company's doorsteps ever again."

"Why, what did I do wrong?"

"For one, you tried to use my son as your pawn to take Flood Industries public. When that didn't work, you used him to invest most of his personal fortune into this company while planning to someday oust him."

"But, but I only did what I thought was the best for the company, it was only business. I never meant to hurt Reese."

"Well, what I'm doing now is what we all here think is best for the company. For me though, it's not business, it's very personal. You have to get up pretty early to fool an old rooster like me, and you failed miserably. I saw through you from the very beginning. And if I can be perfectly honest, I've never liked you. I only tolerated you for his sake anyway. You hurt my son, and no one hurts one of mine without paying a huge price."

I looked everyone there in their eyes and said, "That goes for everyone here. Anyone of you who doesn't want to dance to Flood music should speak up now or forever hold your peace. Because if you ever even think about betraying us, you'll suffer the same fate 'ol Heinrich here has, or worse. Do I make myself crystal clear?"

I continued, "Going forward, this board will report to and receive all directives from Flood Industries, is that understood?" Everyone around the table nodded like bobbleheads. "Ok then. Oh, let's move on Mr. Klaus's motion to vote him CEO."

Everyone screamed a resounding "Nay!"

"The 'nays' carry the motion, Mr. Klaus, you're fired," I said. "Great, and if there's no other new business to cover Mr. Chairman, let's adjourn. Oh, one more thing, a ten percent pay raise for the entire board."

We left to a standing ovation. Everyone, minus Klaus, of course. He just sat there with his head in his hands.

In the limo heading to the airport to fly back home, Reese was looking at his check, smiling and shaking his head. "How did you know what Klaus was planning, Pop? Why didn't you tell me about today?"

"Well, son, the short answer would be we Floods have dealt with folks like that forever. Plus I rely on my gift and our God. When you told us you no longer wanted anything else to do with AQR, I knew your heart's now leading you again. Your brothers made some calls, and all we had to do was attend the meeting. All's well that ends well."

"Amen, Pop. I want to thank the three of you once more."

David put his hand on both of theirs, "We're family, always have been and always will be. It's what we Floods do."

CHAPTER 13

Back at home, life's rolling along pretty smoothly. I mean as smoothly as it can be. I love watching Reese with Phillip, CiCi, Porter and his grandchildren.

He's genuinely happy and doesn't appear to miss the business world at all. He and Kathy are even more than cordial to each other, despite the past enmity of their nasty divorce. Plus, I'm sure his affair with Greta and her being white only made it more painful and embarrassing for her. But they both seem to have put it far behind them. Personally, I wouldn't be surprised if they started courting again.

No one's happier than Phillip, though. He and Reese appear to be joined at the hip. In addition to running the farm together, they travel, fish, bowl and even work out together.

As for me, I'm hanging in there. Don't appear to be any worse or better. Just missing Frankie more and more every passing moment. I piddle around and try to stay busy by reading, walking and even going into town to the parlor on occasion. In addition to witnessing comings and goings, I always look forward to visits from Uncle Clem.

I've gained an even greater measure of respect for him. The fact that he was able to lead this family into his nineties is remarkable in itself, especially, without the gift.

I'm eighty and I feel like I'm a hundred lugging the weight of this old, tired body around. With the family worrying and fretting over me so much now, I often try to hide how I'm really feeling inside. Beverly wants me to get daily checkups, but that's unnecessary. Besides, at this point, I'm positive I'm the best me I can possibly be.

Sometimes the worst storms just seem to come when you least expect them to. The sun can be out, framing a pretty blue sky with a gentle warm breeze, then out of nowhere lightning strikes and life changes you forever.

Phillip was on his motorcycle coming home from visiting his pregnant fiancee'. He was exiting I-20, when a logging truck pulled out in front of him, killing him instantly.

This was another devastating blow, it crushed us all. It also mirrored one of the most painful times of my journey. Seventy years ago, on my tenth birthday, which also happened to be Mama and Pop's twentieth wedding anniversary. Mama surprised Pop with the Harley-Davidson motorcycle he'd always dreamed about. It was by far the happiest moment I'd ever witnessed between them. Smiling ear to ear, he put on his helmet and started the bike. He mounted, waved at Mama and me and took off down the drive. About a quarter mile down the road, there was a loud crash and explosion.

A guy ran the stop sign, struck him and the explosion sent him sailing about twenty feet in the air before hitting his head on the pavement. After his home going, Mama took to her bed, where she remained until her death six months later. She blamed herself, saying she couldn't live without him. She swallowed a lot of pills, washed them down with rum, closed her eyes and joined her beloved. Sadly, to my knowledge, hers was the only suicide our family has ever experienced.

Within a six month span, I was heartbroken and without my parents, but I still had Uncle Clem and Grammy to raise and take care of me. It took a long time for me to wrap my mind around their loss.

We lost Phillip, but would soon be blessed with the birth of his son. Another plus was Reese and Kathy deciding to give their love another try and remarry. I suppose storms always bring blessings as well. They can separate and unite, break you down, then break you through.

CHAPTER 14

Even though CiCi and I are blessed with the sight, we aren't immune to pain. Our hearts ached and we endured and grieved just like everyone else. Some storms take plenty of time to pass through. Some hurts can pierce your heart deeper than others.

I lost a grandson, but CiCi lost her brother, her only sibling. I was more than a little worried about her, and I prayed that she wasn't too overwhelmed. She was a mother who recently gave birth to her second child. Possibly, the child who'll someday beget her successor.

Sometimes, storm clouds seem to hover above you for so long it feels like they'll never pass. The following January, not too long after the birth of Phillip's son, Kathy started feeling ill. Unfortunately, somewhere in the midst of grieving Phillip, she noticed a quarter-sized lump in her left breast. It wasn't long after the biopsy deemed it cancerous that she discovered an even bigger lump in her right breast.

After a few rounds of chemo, radiation and a double mastectomy, she slowly began to recover. Moment by moment, day by day she started to feel like her old self again. Of course, she and Reese both still mourned the loss of their firstborn, but for the first time in a good while, I began to see hope and peace in their eyes again. I was so proud of Reese for being right by his wife's side. He was her biggest supporter every step of the way. It's been truly refreshing to see this part of him again. Being needed and depended on not only encouraged him, but it lightened his mood as well. I think this helped them negotiate their storm of grief - it helped us all, really. Following your heart is always better than being led by your ego.

Depending on how we perceive the storms that are sure to come, they either weaken or buoy our faith. We never see them at first, but blessings are always left in their wake. It's so heartwarming to see that Reese and Kathy are choosing the latter as opposed to the former. I suppose putting the needs of those you love ahead of your own always stems from our hearts, and is what sustains us during the inevitable storms of life.

CiCi has been amazing. As I've said before, our family is in great hands. I love the way she's able to manage the many demands she faces daily: A devoted wife, mother, and daughter; plus being my successor doesn't faze her in the least.

It's definitely made my life easier and I'm even prouder that the entire family respects her and her gift. They've all pledged their eternal support and loyalty to her, and will respectfully follow her leadership. It pleases me because I'm aware of the adoration, honor and love everyone has in their hearts for everyone who's come and gone before them and those who are left to come. God willing, it'll continue through the generations from successor to successor.

Charles R. Butts Jr.

CHAPTER 15

It takes even more effort these days to get around. My energy level ebbs and flows, but hopefully I'll be able to slow the decline some, especially with this being my eighty-first birthday weekend. I'm so tremendously excited the entire family's coming back home to celebrate with me. Not just them, but practically all of my colleagues, close friends, and almost the entire town.

Not having my beloved here to celebrate with me hurts more than a bit, and there were moments I wasn't sure if I'd still be around to see it. Wasn't sure if I even wanted to be. Of course, I'll know when it's time for me to leave. I've promised CiCi I won't go without saying goodbye to her. She, along with Beverly and Bella, have put together a grand affair for me. A concert with some of my favorite music artists, a roast, a huge cookout and fish fry, and a black tie dinner.

With everyone on the way, I prayed and asked God to help me keep it together this weekend. My breath draws a little shorter whenever I get excited, and this past year alone I've had a few fainting spells. Only CiCi knows about them and she promised not to mention it to anyone. I hated asking her to do that, but in time she'll come to understand such things are necessary. They're in the family's best interests. Everyone frets over me enough already, and I don't believe I'd thoroughly enjoy a weekend staring into a sea of worried faces.

All in all, I'm incredibly grateful. Grateful for all God has blessed me with. He's given me sight and wisdom, but experiencing the highest kind of love from my family has been my greatest gift. There's nothing higher or nobler, although you could put time and joy right under love. Until now, I never imagined I could be surrounded by so much love and still feel so all alone.

A little before sunset, the last of the family had arrived, and we were all gathered in the dining room eating supper, fellowshipping and reminiscing. It's moments like these when I miss Frankie the most. Tears well up in my eyes when I look at everyone present and know they exist because of our love and God's favor.

No one appears to be worried about me, though I suspect we're all pretty good at masking what's inside of us sometimes. I promised Beverly I'd have a checkup next week.

The weekend seemed to just fly by, but it was a grand time all around; lots of great food, dancing, and laughter. During the roast, everybody took a turn at really laying it on me. I've always loved a good joke, even if I'm the butt of it. There was whiskey, all kinds of food, and a huge cake for me. Everyone had a great time, and I'll always cherish it. Life is about creating and experiencing memories to tuck away in your heart forever. The highlight of the weekend was watching Reese mend fences with his siblings. That was the best gift I received the entire weekend. I felt great the whole time, Beverly even said I looked and seemed to be doing well. Of course, I had to promise to call her and go to the hospital the next time I started feeling bad. I really didn't feel tired until the weekend was over and everyone was heading back to their homes. Uncle Clem said it best - 'family is everything.'

Charles R. Butts Jr.

CHAPTER 16

My days are filled with all of my favorite things: sunrises, sunsets, walks, fishing, spending quality time and creating happy memories with the family. I'm more than grateful for every moment and every memory. I make myself available for CiCi around her busy schedule. Even with Porter, the kids and work, we manage to sit together alone for a spell to talk.

On occasion, we'll even go down to the trunk to chew the fat with Uncle Clem for a bit. It's not surprising that she loves his stories about the good 'ol days as much as I do. Despite having heard them countless times over the years, they still capture my attention as if I'm hearing them for the first time.

After a haircut and a bite to eat in town, we drove over to the parlor. I had my attorney meet us in my office to go over my will. It was my responsibility to ensure my final wishes (along with the codicil I added earlier) were in place. This would bind my succession plan forever and solidify CiCi as my sole beneficiary and executor.

After all the t's were crossed and i's were dotted, we decided to prepare a couple of bodies. Instead, I watched and assisted her I should say. Though we haven't worked together in years, I'm always amazed at how good she is. If Uncle Clem is the all-time best I've ever seen, CiCi runs a close second.

While driving us back to the farm, CiCi asked, "Are you sure I'll be ready when the time comes?"

"I'm positive. You've been ready for some time now. You're far more advanced than I was when my time came, plus you're younger. Our ancestors know you're ready too, don't you remember them telling you? Trust God, trust them and trust your heart because neither will ever lead you wrong. Trust me, you'll be just fine, ok?"

"Ok, Gramps, I trust you. I just like hearing you say it."

"When my time came, I was scared out of my mind those first few days. I just did my best not to look like I was, but trust me, it'll pass. Just remember you'll never ever be alone."

We made it back to the farm just in time for supper. After dessert, I sat in the courtyard watching a beautiful sunset with some premium whiskey and a cigar fresh from the humidor.

Just taking in God's beauty and shuffling some of my old memories and thoughts around. Nowadays, I sleep so soundly I'm sometimes unable to catch every sunrise. Even so, I'm all the more grateful for everything I'm able to see, hear, touch, feel and taste. I may not be as I once was, but I'm still being, doing, appreciating and loving everything and every beautiful moment I'm blessed with.

Charles R. Butts Jr.

CHAPTER 17

Clement and David came to town for a few days to visit and bring me up to speed about some potential acquisitions. After reaching consensus to move forward on some projects, David invited Clement and Reese to come to Atlanta with him. The Hawks were playing in the finals, and David wanted to show his brothers the entire operation. Surprisingly, they opted to drive instead of flying up there. I had an uneasy feeling about their trip come over me where I couldn't shake the foreboding of another approaching storm.

In the fourscore and the one year I've journeyed on this side of the sun, I've learned to trust my instincts. But out of respect for my sons' excitement of being and traveling together, I kept it to myself. I

83

believe everyone must be allowed to choose their path and make their own decisions every moment they're here, but that's every adult moment I mean. Be it a positive or negative outcome, every moment provides growth and ultimately serves to teach us.

Nearly a week later, in the middle of the night, on the drive back to the farm, there was a terrible accident. With Clement and David asleep, Reese dozed off at the wheel. When he opened his eyes, he overcorrected, swerved off the road and crashed head-on into a tree. For whatever reason, Clement wasn't wearing his seatbelt. Reese and David suffered minor injuries, but Clement was ejected from the car and suffered a terrible fall. He fractured a couple of vertebrae in his back. He was airlifted to Druid City Memorial, where we would later learn he was paralyzed from his waist down. David blamed himself for inviting them, and Reese blamed himself for causing the accident and was overwhelmed with guilt. His prognosis was grim. Every doctor and specialist we brought in said Clement would never walk again.

Even going through a storm as terrible as this one, blessings of sunlight pierced through the dark clouds. There's always a silver lining and sliver of hope to be found if you look hard enough.

Despite being the one paralyzed, Clement consoled his brothers. He said it was just an accident and no one was the blame. He vowed not only to walk again but insisted on still running the day to day operations.

I knew he and David would be ok, but Reese has come off the rails a bit. He's grown more sullen, isolated and drinking a lot. We have to find a way to reach him before it's too late. I fear he's rapidly spiraling into a darkness that very few people are able to escape on their own. I can barely see the light and sparkle in his eyes, and that's what troubles me most.

CHAPTER 18

Clement and Lisa, along with their kids, spouses and grandkids in tow, relocated to the farm to live. They thought his convalescence would go smoother down here. Determined to walk again, Clement furiously attacked his rehab and therapy. When he wasn't doing that, he continued guiding Flood Industries to exponential growth. Of course, he oversees everything while grooming and mentoring all of the grandchildren on their positions and duties with the company. Since his childhood, I could always tell that he's the most driven and purposeful child I have. That says a lot because they all possess an incredible drive and work ethic in everything they do.

The difference between Reese and my other children was they always put God and our family legacy above business. They chose to still honor our ancestors, while never seeking personal gratification and gain for themselves.

Reese was maniacal at succeeding, no matter the cost and for all the credit. With his downward spiral escalating, we're all doing whatever we can to lift his spirits.

Another New Year arrived, and true to his word, Clement took his first unassisted steps and began walking again. Nothing can stop a determined Flood! Seeing Clement walk again, seemed to lift Reese's spirits some. I can clearly see he's not carrying so much guilt around anymore.

He smiles, laughs and interacts with everyone more often. I'm still a bit troubled that he can't seem to get his drinking under control. He won't admit it, but I believe he misses the corporate world more than he thought he would. And if I were a betting man, I'd say he's been feeling the itch to return to it more and more.

CHAPTER 19

A couple of months later, we had a huge party here at the farm celebrating both Clement's birthday and him walking again. During the celebration, when no one was paying attention, Reese got behind the wheel and slipped away from the farm. No one really knew he was missing until we got a call from the sheriff's department. He was found near the town square around midnight, with his car still running and asleep at the wheel.

Naturally, he failed the breathalyzer and field sobriety tests. I was so grateful and relieved no one was hurt. Had he actually been driving, he could have possibly injured himself or someone else. Arrested and charged with DUI, me and Clement went to town to post bail and bring him home. Embarrassed, he apologized and sobbed the entire ride back.

The following afternoon, and with Reese still upstairs sleeping it off, Kathy and CiCi gathered everyone together in the parlor. We all wanted to come up with a suitable plan of action for him to get the help he so desperately needs.

We reached consensus on an intervention. CiCi and Kathy made arrangements beforehand for Reese to be sent to the best facility in Atlanta. After supper, the top counselor at the treatment facility joined us to meet with Reese. We all would get a chance to tell him how much his drinking affects all of us.

When Reese came and took a seat in the parlor, we all took turns reading the impact statements we'd written for him. Kathy and CiCi went first, then Porter, followed by his brothers and sisters. I went last. It was very emotional, everyone shed tears because of the respect and unconditional love we have for him. In the end, though, he tearfully agreed to enter the treatment program. He even insisted on the ninety-day program. Wiping away his tears, he apologized and vowed to everyone he'd do his best to conquer his addiction.

As we all stood outside watching him leave, we all felt hopeful and a little better.

CHAPTER 20

Three months later, Reese returned home from the treatment center. He looked really healthy and well rested, I could see the sparkle in his eyes again. He was more than determined to maintain his sobriety. He attended his local AA meetings religiously and stayed in contact with his sponsor. He even agreed to continue with outpatient therapy.

Before he came home, his counselors at the center thought employment would be a tremendous help in his recovery and overall well-being. Collectively, we voted and decided to give him a position with the company. We figured it would add stability and give him purpose. We assigned him VP of procurement and acquisitions. He won't hold any shares of stock or voting privileges, nor will he be authorized to make decisions. Other than that, his only condition was to report to Clement and any prospective acquisition recommendation from him needed unanimous approval from the board.

If I'm honest, I must admit I haven't been feeling well for some time now. It almost feels as if the extra energy I expend pretending to be well makes it worse. CiCi and I were under the greenhouse chewing the fat with Uncle Clem when I started feeling a little strange. I felt dizzy and flush with heat, and my hands and feet started tingling and trembling. That's the last thing I remembered before waking up in a room in Druid City Hospital hooked up to monitors. CiCi was sitting bedside holding my hand.

"Welcome back, Gramps. I'm so glad to see you open your eyes."

"What happened?"

"You had a mild heart attack two days ago. Let me go get Auntie Beverly and the rest of them. We've all been praying nonstop since you collapsed."

"Ok, Baby Girl." Bella and my sons followed Beverly into my room. While she checked my vitals, the others surrounded my bed. It really made this old, tired man feel good. The fact that I didn't see Uncle Clem (or anyone else from the other side) made me feel a little better. Not that I'm afraid to leave or anything like that, I know it's coming sooner or later.

Beverly took my hand and said, "Your vitals look real good, Daddy, but I'd like for you to stay here a few more days. We need to run more tests. I insist, Doctor's orders."

"Whatever you say, Baby Girl."

Bella pecked me on the cheek and said, "Thank God you are ok, Daddy. Please don't ever scare us like this anymore."

"I'll do my best not to. I promise."

Reese, Clement and David took their turns hugging me and saying they love me as well.

"Listen, I'll be fine, I'm a tough 'ol bird. I love all of you, and I'm so proud to be your father. Anyone else out there?"

Laughing, everyone said in unison, "The whole family!"

After hugs, kisses, and handshakes from the family, I ate a little jello before drifting off to sleep again. Since I can't remember passing out, I must be sleeping pretty well these days. After a couple of more days of resting and testing, I was discharged and allowed to go home. They didn't have to tell me twice, I've never been more excited to get out of there. Can't wait to get back to the home place, I even hear it calling me.

Charles R. Butts Jr.

CHAPTER 21

There's no place like home. Still on the mend from the heart attack, I'm carefully monitored and fussed over daily. So much so that the only time I think I'm alone is when I'm sleeping or in the bathroom. Even then, I'm confident someone's near and either watching or listening in on me.

My every meal is carefully prepared, and I sure do miss my whiskey and cigars. I am walking and exercising more though, and as a result, I've dropped a few pounds.

I must admit though, physically I'm feeling much better. Other than the strict diet and exercise, I read, listen to my jazz, play checkers and watch TV. I suppose the best part about this situation is spending even more time with CiCi, Uncle Clem, and even some of the others on occasion.

At least now I'm beyond convinced the family will continue to thrive long after I'm gone. They've weathered some of the worst storms, but they know if they keep the faith, it'll only be temporary. They've discovered firsthand that God never leaves us either. If He brings us to a storm, He'll undoubtedly bring us through it. I'm just so grateful for everything He's blessed me with, and all He's allowed me to experience.

Reese seems to be doing well on all fronts. From all I've been told and what I've seen myself, he's very happy and his life finally appears to have balance. He even spends more of his time with his family than he does working, if you can believe that. He's more involved with our charities, even with community service and church.

I'm equally proud of his efforts and accomplishments. Don't know how much time I have left, but I'm very proud; just thinking about the generations yet to warm this old man's heart.

But through every storm and every subsequent triumph, things just aren't the same since I lost my Frankie. That's one storm that probably won't pass until I do. I can continue trying to put on a brave face and pretend things are the same, but I'm positive I'm not fooling anyone anymore - especially myself.

Sure, I have the love, loyalty and support of an amazing family and incredible friends, but she's irreplaceable. I miss her touch, I miss holding her and being held by her. I miss her smile and laughter as well. Whenever I'm feeling low, I just reach down deep into my heart and pull out an amazing memory we created during our fifty years together.

On our wedding night, she told me she knew I'd be her husband even before she picked me up from the airport. She was my peace, my everything. I've never been loved like that before, and I've never loved someone like that either. Everyone should be blessed with a love like that. So even surrounded by a house full of family that loves me dearly, I grow even lonelier by the minute.

Charles R. Butts Jr.

CHAPTER 22

Summer swept us up in its rhythm, and before long, Autumn's frost graced us. The day before Halloween, trouble brewed in town, and once again the tragic winds of a mighty storm began blowing.

From his desk at work one day, Porter watched his comrades chasing an armed man on foot. Without thinking, he joined the pursuit, and as he was closing in on him, the perpetrator turned and fired a couple of shots. One bullet hit him in the stomach, and the other one barely nicked the femoral artery of his right leg.

Fortunately, they got him to the hospital in time. However, because he's been more of an administrator and no longer patrolling the streets, he wasn't wearing a vest. Even still, and with much prayer, the surgery went well, but he faced a lengthy recovery.

Once again, CiCi was more than amazing during this crisis. There was no doubt that she is more than capable of succeeding me. In some ways, it almost felt like watching them carry on without me. I can't even begin to state how proud I was.

Like all great leaders, she possesses this incredible ability of compartmentalizing her emotions. With her, the glass is always overflowing with faith and courage.

Certainly, she was scared and more than concerned for her husband, but as usual, she was also the calm, that quelled the storm for all of us. She took care of him and their kids while continuing to lead us forward without missing a beat. Naturally, everyone was worried and upset, but the prayers of the entire town and God's grace brought him through.

A few months later, Porter was back on his feet. I suppose this incident caused him to reevaluate his priorities in life because he promptly resigned from the sheriff's department. He took me up on my offer for a safer position within the family. He agreed to sign on as head of security operations for the entire farm.

The rewards were twofold; Porter got to spend all the time he wanted with CiCi and the kids, (they've never seemed happier) plus, he still found purpose doing something he's always loved to do. I haven't seen this much romance around here since Frankie and me. And I, for one, couldn't be any happier for them.

I've grown even more tired now. I'm never up now before the late morning or mid-afternoon. Bedtime depends on how long I've been up that day. Sometimes, when I've slept in, I stay up late staring at the beautiful night sky or listening to its stillness. Sometimes, I feel as though I'm drifting between this world and the next.

I chose to never ask great-grandpa about how this time was for him. I want to experience it first hand and find out on my own. Besides, I'm almost positive he wouldn't have told me anyhow. This way, I remain fully present during every sensation of every experience. Life is for living in the now.

My goal is to continue to do so. My time is near. Most folks hold on as tightly to what they know as life for as long as they can. They do so mainly out of fear, without realizing life is all there is. Me, on the other hand, I look forward to reuniting with my wife and beginning our forevermore.

Charles R. Butts Jr.

CHAPTER 23

I'm weary and just plain run down now. Every step I take weighs me down like I'm dragging a ton. Practically all sunrises and sunsets are viewed from my room, and that's only if I'm even awake to see them. I spend the majority of my time in bed now. Even still, I'm hardly ever alone. Seems like the entire family has moved to the farm, sensing I don't have much time left on this side of the river.

All the fretting doesn't even bother me because I'm not going anywhere just yet. I still manage to get outside for some fresh air every now and then.

Most of the time, I wait until the wee hours of the morning to go under the greenhouse. I still like swallowing a snootful of whiskey and puffing a stogie on occasion. Surprisingly, I believe it helps me. I feel more energetic afterwards.

Even if anyone's aware of me sneaking down here, they love and respect me enough not to say anything. Besides, I'm still their father, grandpa and great-grandpa, and none of them would be here without me.

I was putting out my cigar and getting ready to go back to the house early one morning when Uncle Clem showed up.

"Hey, son, how's it going?"

"Hey, Unc, it's going. I'm still here, though I strongly suspect not too much longer. My winter has given me an even higher respect for you, if that's even possible. How'd you do it for so long?"

After chuckling a bit, he said, "Our situations were different, son, I had a charge to keep. Nothing and no one was going to stop me from keeping it. I couldn't leave until you were ready to take over. In your case though, CiCi's been more than ready for a long time. She's actually already on the job. I expect every successor to have it easier than their predecessor, which is the way it should be. It's the natural order of things."

"You're right, I'm so proud of her too. Knowing the family will continue to love each other, prosper and weather any storm it'll face, has given me an indescribable peace."

"You've done exceptionally well son, we're all so very proud of you. You should be proud of yourself," he added.

"Not proud Unc, just content, satisfied and, of course, tired."

"I knew you had it in you all along. You're a Flood, and this is what we do. Every last one of us on the other side are so proud of all of you."

"Thanks again. Guess I better head on back. I know they'll come looking for me. I just wanted a drink and a smoke. The bonus was spending some time with you."

"Ok son, I'll be seeing you."

"Bye now."

I made it all the way back to my room without anyone knowing I'd been gone. It took more time and effort than before, but eventually I got there.

Charles R. Butts Jr.

CHAPTER 24

Despite witnessing countless of souls leaving this world, I'm unsure how they genuinely feel inside when they're nearing the river. For me though, it's almost as if time has slowed significantly and I'm one with everything; the sun, moon, wind, air, trees, animals, and of course, people. It's like, for the first time on my journey, I can hear and feel mother earth's pulse and share every breath she takes.

The irony is you're too old to do anything else but take notice. It's all you have energy for. God's wisdom truly fascinates me.

To be part of such a creation is an honor. Every breeze, blade of grass, leaf or bee pollinating a flower, is such a wondrous sight to behold. Life's picture becomes crystal clear and you understand its purpose.

We come here, blessed with free will so that God may be expressed through our actions. Every negative and positive experience we've had has gifted us with lessons and subtle reminders of our connection to Him.

I tire very easily now, but that secret's been long out of the bag. Eating, sleeping and even talking takes great effort. Then out of the blue, Kathy's cancer came back. It's metastasized and seized all of her vital organs. Other than curbing the pain and making her as comfortable as possible, nothing more can be done. I truly admire her strength and courage. She says she's not afraid of what's to come, in fact, she welcomes it. She's ready to escape her painful and cancer-riddled body. Sometimes, I hold her hand, read to her and answer any questions to the best of my ability. As usual, I'm more than proud of my family. Everyone's taking their turn to say their goodbyes.

CiCi is our constant calm during this storm and a pillar of strength, but unfortunately, Reese was not so much. His state of mind troubles me. He's using alcohol to try to cope with the guilt he's feeling. He believes things might have been different if he'd never left her in the first place. He has it in his mind that their nasty divorce began to weaken her and it's all his fault. CiCi and I have tried to convince him it isn't, but he won't believe us. I've even heard Kathy tell him, but he's still inconsolable.

Two weeks later, Kathy passed away. CiCi and I watched her leave with some of her folks. Homegoing preparations are underway, and Reese is trying with all his might to hold it all together. Later that evening after supper, I sat him down and tried to offer some words of comfort.

"Son, I know it hurts bad, believe me I know. But trust me, she's in a greater place and you'll see her again. I promise."

"I know that Pop, but I'm sad about all the time we lost. We could have created even more memories."

"I know son, we can always second guess ourselves and wonder what we could have done differently. What you could have done to keep her here. But there's nothing you, me, CiCi or anyone else could have done to change the outcome. Want to know why?"

"Why, Pop?"

"Because she was never ours to begin with, son. She belongs to God - we all do. He's our creator and He wanted her back home. Just like He'll call us all home someday. I promise you, it'll be a glorious day indeed."

"I just wish I could see her and talk to her one last time. It's times like these when I envy you and CiCi the most."

"Don't be so quick to want to take a walk in our shoes, son. We would argue that makes it even more painful, I'm proof of that. Try not to focus on what may have been. Instead, focus on what's going to be and how you're going to feel when you reunite someday. That's what I hold on to, and what I'm looking forward to the most. Time doesn't heal or lessen the pain, it just makes it more bearable."

"I guess you're right Pop. I'll try my best."

"That's all the Lord asks of us."

"Well, thanks for making me feel a little better about this," he said.

"Thanks for listening and allowing me to. Never forget that life never ends."

In typical Flood fashion, Kathy had a fantastic homegoing, I'm told. I stayed at the farm greeting and mingling with the guests. Didn't have the strength to attend the actual service and burial, but my heart and spirit were there with them.

CHAPTER 25

Still reeling from Kathy's passing, the kids called a family meeting. Since everyone's still here, I thought it was a great idea. Even though CiCi controls my shares and my proxy now, it made me feel good that my kids still valued my input.

Clement gaveled and called the meeting to order, and after reading the minutes from the last meeting and financial reports, they all turned towards me. Clement stood and said, "Pops, we called this meeting for a couple of reasons. First, just to thank you for all you've accomplished, and all you've taught us." I felt my eyes water as they all hugged me and told me how much they respect and love me.

"The second reason is, effective immediately, we your children are all retiring. While working and building with you and Mom gave us purpose, we want to shift all our energy towards family now. We've witnessed enough examples to know life can be fleeting and no one is promised tomorrow. We know spending as much time as possible with family is the most important thing in life. Our kids and grandkids have been running Flood Industries for some time now anyway. They're more than capable of taking the business to higher and higher heights. We'll always be just a phone call away if they should need us. We just wanted your blessing on this."

"By all means retire," I said, "you don't need my blessing. I'm so happy for all of you. It's my fondest wish for you all to spend the rest of your lives traveling and experiencing all that life has to offer. I'm sure your Mother would feel the same way. But, since we're all here, I want you all to know that as of last week, CiCi controls my shares. Plus, I decreed that Flood Industries must always remain a private, family-owned entity and can never be sold. It's not an issue of trust, it's because of a sworn promise that's lasted for generations. It must continue to do so forever because it's bigger than all of us. No one here started Flood Industries, so none of us have any rights to ever sell it. Agreed?"

They smiled and shouted "agreed" in unison.

"Now, if there's no more business to discuss, let's adjourn. I need a nap," I said.

After my nap, I was sitting on the bench in the cemetery, when Reese joined me. After placing flowers on Kathy's grave and saying a prayer, he sat down beside me.

"Hey, son, how's it going?" I asked.

"Hey, Pop, I'm hanging in there. I just miss her so much."

"I know exactly how you feel. Reach in that huge heart of yours and pull out a happy memory you two created and shared. That always makes me feel better. I was so proud of you earlier today. The old you was once addicted to the excitement of the business world."

"You said it right, that was the old me. All I care about now is family. It sickens me to remember how I used to be."

"Don't look at it that way, son. If you were never how you used to be, you couldn't appreciate how you are now."

"I suppose that makes sense. When I think about the pain and disappointment I've caused others, I get so angry at myself. I think about all of my failures and shortcomings, too. Sometimes, I allow those thoughts to take me to a dark place."

"That's nonsense son, you must always forgive and love yourself. There are countless others in this world who've done far worse than you, trust me. God brought you to and through all those storms for a reason. Each storm brings a lesson and leaves you better because of it. Truth be told, I believe they distance us farther from our ego and draw us nearer to Him. Just like you thank God for bringing you through, don't forget to give thanks and praise while going through. I know sometimes it feels like life is unfair, but it's really not. It always offers you far more than it'll ever take from you."

"You're right. Pop. I've never looked at life that way before."

"Always remember, while we'll never be perfect, the God inside us always is. Hold on to Him when times get dark. Ok?"

"Will do Pop. Thanks. I'm going to town for a haircut. See you later."

"Ok son. Be safe."

CHAPTER 26

My kids are really enjoying their retirement. The postcards are coming in from all over the world. When they're not traveling, family, friends and hobbies take up the rest of their time. I think it's great because that means they have less time to fuss over me. Physically, there's been no change, I'm just grateful to still be able to care for myself even though it may take longer than it used to. Truth be told, that's fine with me - I'm in no hurry to do anything. All that remains for me is time, and something tells me I don't have too much of it left.

Reese is the only one who appears anxious and on edge about being retired. Unfortunately, he's always been pretty restless. He's never taken the time to appreciate the blessings and beauty unfolding around him each day. He's drinking again, which gives me cause for concern. Plus, with CiCi and Porter's added responsibilities, he doesn't get to see them or his grandchildren as much as he'd like to.

In a weird way, I believe he now understands how CiCi and Phillip must have felt about him when they were growing up. To stay somewhat busy, he's trying his hand at day trading stocks, but his losses continue to mount more and more daily. At the rate he's going, he'll lose a massive chunk of his money.

He's been keeping a low profile lately. Besides losing huge amounts of money, he drank too much one night and got behind the wheel again. He swerved off the road and crashed head-on to a tree. Had he not been wearing his seat belt, the crash probably would have killed him.

He walked away without a scratch, was arrested, highly embarrassed and filled with guilt. However, he refused to go back to the treatment facility. But fortunately, he's agreed to more outpatient therapy and treatment.

That, and a couple of months in jail and three hundred hours of community service the court imposed on him. I can't tell if it'll work or not, but I'm not sure anyone else can either. I don't believe I can reach him anymore.

It's like my words fall on deaf ears whenever I try to talk to him. I just want him to know how much I love him and I'm always in his corner. I want only the highest and best for him. But it's not enough for me to want it for him, he has to want it for himself.

Besides praying, I don't know what more I can do for him. But what I won't do is enable or pity him. I had all the alcohol removed from the house, and changed all of the codes under the greenhouse. He's at a meeting now, but maybe I'll see if he wants to go fishing after supper.

CHAPTER 27

Reese came to supper reeking of alcohol. He was slurring his words and speaking so rapidly, we could barely understand what he was saying. This was the first time I saw both fear and shame in CiCi's eyes as her tears fell.

"Daddy, please get some help! Please! If you won't do it for us, do it for Mom. She wouldn't want to see you carrying on like this!" CiCi said.

"Like what, Baby Girl?" Reese replied.

"Unable to straighten up and get yourself together. She always told me you were a fighter, and fighting is in our blood. We never quit, we always pick ourselves up. We fight and keep moving forward."

"I know, and you're absolutely right. I just feel like a huge failure. I broke her heart once, and I wasn't the best father I could possibly be to you and Phillip. Then once I realized what's most important in life, I lose two huge pieces of my heart; three, counting your grandma. It's just so hard for me to forgive myself, and even harder to rid myself of all this pain. I don't believe it'll ever end."

"It will end, Daddy, especially if you want it to. Seems to me, you're too focused on the past. Be grateful for what you still are a part of now. Forgive yourself, let go of yesterday's past and join us here and now. Can you do that for us? For me? Will you at least promise us you'll try?"

"Ok. Not only will I try for myself, but I vow to make an effort for all of you. Forgive me, and I'll forgive myself."

"That's my father who's speaking to us now. Listen to how clear and sober you sound now!"

"You're right, Baby Girl, can I have a hug? How did you get to be so smart?"

"I'm not sure if I am Daddy, but I come from generations of wise people."

"Indeed you do, Baby Girl. Now if y'all will excuse me, I'm going upstairs to shower, shave and get some rest. Good night."

We all bade him good night and watched him go up the stairs to his room. Watching CiCi quieting storms and putting out fires is a thing of beauty. The legacy of love she'll leave this family will be both monumental and eternal.

CHAPTER 28

Now that I believe everyone's asleep, it's the perfect time to make my way over to the greenhouse. I'll finally have that cigar and sip of whiskey I've been craving since supper. I've always loved the quiet and stillness of a late night. It's one of the things I'm sure I'll miss the most. Bright stars, a shimmering moon, and a slight breeze make a beautiful night.

When I make it to the greenhouse, I notice it's unlocked. When I get on the elevator, I can hear music blaring from below. When I get to the bottom and the elevator opens, I see Reese. His back is facing me as he reaches for another jar of moonshine. Judging by how loudly he's singing the song's lyrics and the empty jar already on the table, he must be pretty drunk. When I turned the music off, he turned, faced me and asked,

"Pop, what are you doing here? I figured I'd have the place to myself this time of night. You shouldn't be here, I need to be alone."

"I'm here because I want to know why you're not keeping your word. You promised all of us you're going back to the treatment center."

"Yeah, I know, but just like I failed the last time, I figured I'd eventually fail again. I just decided to cut to the chase. Admit it, Pop, I'm a failure! I'm a failure and all I've ever done was disappoint you and Mom! I'm tired, Pop, I'm just tired of it all!"

"Listen to me, son, you are not a failure, nor have you ever been. Trying something and failing at it doesn't make you a failure. Refusing to ever try again after you fail does make you a failure, though. Everyone fails son, it's a part of the journey. You're a great husband, son, father, brother, uncle, grandfather, and businessman."

"Come on Pop, you don't expect me to believe you've always felt this way about me. Do you?"

"Son, listen to me, I'm telling you the truth. There's no doubt we've had our fair share of differences and misunderstandings over the years, but it's never stopped me from loving and being proud of you. Storms of disappointment and failure will find us all, but if you remain grateful while going through them, they'll always leave a lesson behind and a rainbow on the other side. Do you hear me, son?"

"Pop, I'm not trying to hear any of that feel-good Flood folklore right now! I'm way too tired for that! Sometimes, the pain a storm brings is so great it never passes and you never escape it." He reached into his right pocket and pulled out a pearl-handled forty-five pistol and points it at me.

"What are you doing, son? Please put that pistol down and let's talk about it. Do you really want to shoot your eighty-one-year-old father?"

He then pulled an identical pistol from his other pocket, held it to his temple and said, "That depends on you, Pop. If you take one step towards me, yell for help or do anything to stop me, I'll shoot you first, then myself. Please don't move, Pop. God knows I don't want to hurt you. If you do as I ask, I'll just shoot myself. Either way, my failures and pain end right here and right now."

I felt my heart beating faster and became flush with heat. Suddenly, the room filled with light. Uncle Clem, Grandpa, Grammy, Great-Grandpa and Great-Grandma along with Mom and Pop appeared. None of them uttered a word. Despite the tense situation, they were all smiling. I didn't know what to do.

Clutching my chest I said, "Son, only God gives life and sends us to this world, and He alone takes us from this world in His own time. That time was decided long before you were formed in your Mother's womb. Let's talk about this. You can come back to the company if you like. You are your thoughts son, never allow fear of failure to consume them."

"It's too late Pop, I'm way past done," he said.

"Think about CiCi and your grandkids. How do you think they're going to feel?"

"Just tell them, my sisters, brothers, nieces, nephews, and even Porter that I'm so sorry, and I love them all dearly. Lastly, I love you so much, Pop. Don't blame yourself, I couldn't have asked for a better father or mother. I've always wanted to please you and be just like you. I tried to wear and carry our name with pride and honor, but I suppose that was too big of a burden for me to try to bear."

"I am proud son, please put the guns down!"

"Sorry, Pop."

He put the pistol pointed at me on the table, and in a split second, squeezed the trigger of the pistol pointed at his temple. Blood and brain matter splattered all over me and against the wall. Reese collapsed and fell to the floor. Helpless, despondent and cradling him in my arms I screamed, "Noooooooooooooo!"

CHAPTER 29

Again, I awoke to beeping monitors and hooked up to all kinds of tubes. I couldn't remember much but prayed that the glimpses of memories speckled about in my mind weren't true. Moments later, I learned my fears were real. Reese had taken his life in the greenhouse that night, and I'd been comatose after suffering another mild heart attack because of it. Later that evening, while I was still trying to recollect and piece together everything that happened, CiCi and the kids entered the room.

Reese's home going had been held earlier, because they all were still wearing their funeral garb. Maybe it was for the best that I've been unconscious these past days. I'm sure it's the only reason I'm still here. It's definitely something I didn't want to see.

CiCi sat on the edge of my bed, smiled and said, "Hey Gramps, welcome back. You gave us another scare, but we're so happy to see you open your eyes again."

"You mean it's true Baby Girl? I was praying that everything was just part of a bad dream. Another piece of my heart is gone, and I didn't get a chance to say goodbye. Well, at least for now anyway. I'm sure all of you took great care in giving him a proper Flood send-off, didn't you?"

Taking my hand in hers as tears streamed from her eyes, she said, "We did indeed Gramps. We did everything you would have wanted us too. We interred Daddy's remains in the crypt he had built for him and Mom. A lot of well-wishers and close friends were paying their respects and offering their condolences too. Practically, the whole town and most of the business world. Even Heinrich, Ingrid and Greta attended and offered their support. They wanted to visit you."

"That's great to hear - who came for him?"

"Gram, great-grandpa and great-grandma too." My spirits lightened immensely when she said Frankie came back.

"What was she like Baby Girl? What did she say? Did she leave a message for me or anything?" I distinctly remember her telling me she wouldn't until it's my time to cross the river.

"She said she struggled with the decision, but because it was y'all's child and since you were comatose, she felt compelled to come and stand in the gap for your son."

"What does she look like? I bet she's still as beautiful as ever."

"She is Gramps. She looks like she did when you two first started dating and she's still as sassy as ever."

"How long have I been here? How long was I unconscious?"

"You been here about five days. Auntie says your coma was medically induced. Both the cardiology team and Auntie Beverly believed that was the best course of action for your prognosis."

"I suppose they were right." So, while Beverly and the cardiology team were probing and prodding, everybody came in and took turns telling me how much they love me. But what made me feel even better and resonated deep in my soul, was knowing we'd made it through and survived the worst of another storm. That and knowing I'll be going home in another week or so.

Charles R. Butts Jr.

CHAPTER 30

Acouple of weeks later after a complete battery of tests from head to toe, I was discharged and brought home. And of course, I insisted the first stop being our family cemetery. Because I missed his home going, I really needed to visit Reese's crypt. I desperately hoped that sooner or later he'd visit so we could talk.

There's a strangeness that I suppose every parent who survives their child goes through. The world seems and feels indescribably unnatural somehow, and you can definitely feel the void of losing another piece of your soul. My heart grieves for his spirit because I feel I failed him. I thought I did everything I possibly could for him, and maybe I did. Even so, it's been very challenging to remove this shroud of guilt and pain that envelops me.

I've been replaying everything we've experienced together these past few years. But it only saddens me more. I suppose some things can only be explained and made clear by the person who is the source of my grief. I was down in the greenhouse for a smoke and a drink when Uncle Clem showed up.

"Hey son, how's my favorite nephew doing? How are you holding up?"

"Hard to tell Unc. I know how life works, and I know everyone has their own journey. I guess I'd just feel better if I knew why it happened. This was something I wouldn't wish on anyone. Why did he feel it was necessary to take his own life? He was surrounded by the people who loved him the most, and I can't seem to shake the feeling that maybe there was something else I could have done to prevent it."

"Are you hearing yourself son? You just said everyone has to follow their own path. Try to accept that it was his choice. You and Frankie were wonderful parents to him, and he'd be the first to say so. Life just is sometimes what we fear the most happens. When it does, all you can do is grieve and move on. You already know where he is, so try to forgive yourself and move on. Remember, as long as you're here, you're the leader of this family and everyone still looks to you for guidance."

"You're right as usual Unc. Again, it just reminds me of how strong you had to be despite everything you faced. You lost Aunt Lizzie Ruth and Cynthia, yet you kept moving forward."

"It's not easy son and believe me. I was hurt and grieved every loss during every storm I faced. But no storm lasts forever. Strength comes in many forms. Grief can either make the strong stronger or can weaken the weak even more. Draw your strength from CiCi and the family, and they'll draw their strength from you. It's love, togetherness and faith that guides families through storms."

"As usual Unc, you've made me feel a whole lot better. Thanks."

"There's no need to thank me son. Besides, if I made you feel better, just imagine how you'll feel after this." When I turned away, I was face to face with Reese. For the first time in a long time, he looked really happy.

"Hey Pop."

"Hey son, how are you? I've been hoping to run into you ever since you left."

"I'm great Pop. I've been in your heart the whole time where I'll always remain. I wanted to give you a little time to heal first. I'm so sorry for all the pain I've caused you. I want you to know that no one is to blame. It was my choice and my choice alone. I was in a dark place, and my heart was too heavy to bear another ounce of pain. I just didn't want to hurt anymore. But as you can see, I'm more than ok. I'm here to ask for your forgiveness, and to thank you for loving me so much. I'm also asking you to move forward with our family, they still need you. Plus, I have a message to deliver from Mom. She wants you to know that she loves and misses you so very much. She said she's looking forward to seeing you again. But there's no rush, because, as you know better than most, time doesn't exist on our side."

"Thank you, son. There's nothing to forgive. Seeing you reminded me of whom you really are and whom we really belong to. It's been one of my life's greatest honors to be your father. Tell your mother I feel the exact same way." I looked at them both and said, "Thank you for reminding me about God's wisdom and love. I feel a thousand times better, even better physically. We'll see each other again." They both smiled as Uncle Clem said, "Count on it."

After they faded through the wall, I headed for the house. My spirits were so high, I felt like taking the stairs.

CHAPTER 31

Nearing summer's end, it was time for Sterling to go back to school. Usually, he's rambunctious and bursting with enthusiasm, and can hardly wait to go back. Something doesn't sit right in my spirit about him.

He hasn't been himself lately. He hasn't been running around, climbing trees, swimming, riding his bike or any of the things a healthy nine-year-old boy would be doing. CiCi and Porter are saying its normal, just nothing more than growing pains.

But after I described his mood and lack of activity to Beverly, she called CiCi and suggested they bring him up to Druid City in

Tuscaloosa for some tests. She thinks she knows what's wrong with him but wants to be sure and thoroughly dissects his lab reports before confirming his diagnosis.

Beverly, after consulting with some of the premier pediatric oncologists in the country diagnosed Sterling with acute lymphoblastic leukemia. It was a stunning blow for us all, but CiCi's attitude didn't surprise me in the least. She immediately declared victory over it and asked Beverly about treatment options.

Beverly gave CiCi and Porter a couple of options; chemo or a bone marrow transplant. She went on to say that because since he's just at stage one, she recommends the bone marrow transplant. She also said finding a match may take some time because of Sterling's rare blood type.

Believe it or not, there wasn't a match in our entire family. Even after searching the national registry, we couldn't locate a match. I hadn't been tested though, wasn't even considered. I don't know if it's because of my age or my recent health problems, but Sterling needs help now, so I insisted on being tested. Besides, the next one with the gift of sight can only come through Sterling or P.J.

As fate and faith would have it, my marrow was deemed to be a perfect match. I insisted that they begin withdrawing it from me at once and transplanting it into Sterling. They were more than a little concerned for me, but they all understood the importance.

I was a pretty sore afterward, but the transplant was a huge success. Sterling's white blood cell count was restored and before long, he was in full remission. Before my procedure, I thought it would be prudent to take more than the usual amount of marrow.

I don't know how much time I have left, plus they'll have more stored should it return after I'm gone. Even after I healed, I suggested they go in and get even more.

Sterling quickly recovered, and before long he was back to his old running and jumping self. Once again, he had tons of energy and before long, he was back in his tree house swinging from a rope. That's the way it should be. Faith has never failed me or was unable to carry me through. Even through this storm, I felt pretty good - and knowing Sterling's going to be fine makes me feel even better. Everything must be overcome in the present for our family to secure its future.

CHAPTER 32

We've always been a close-knit family, but I suppose Sterling's illness has further strengthened our family ties. Standing firmly together through tough times and leaning on one another will do that.

The entire gang's back home this Labor Day weekend. Since everybody's back for the cookout, CiCi and Porter thought they'd make the weekend even more memorable by renewing their vows. Their ten years together seems to have flown by.

The ceremony was amazing. Watching them standing at the altar hand in hand, looking at each other so lovingly was beautiful.

They always remind me of Frankie and me. The highlight of the entire ceremony had to be seeing Sterling proudly escort his mother down the aisle. And of course, there were a lot of guests. Uncle Clem brought a handful of folks with him. I recognized most of them, but a few of them weren't familiar at all.

After the ceremony, and before the reception, CiCi and I went down into the greenhouse to meet with our people. Reese walked up to CiCi, smiled and said, "Congratulations Sweet Girl! Your mom and I are so happy for you and Porter. I've apologized to Pop, but I feel obligated to apologize to you too. You look so beautiful and are so very special. I regret so very much not being there for you and your brother when you were little and needed me the most. I'm so sorry for everything."

"It's ok Dad, there's no need to apologize. Phillip and I never lacked any love or support. Gramps and Gram always made sure we always had more than enough. You're my father, and I'll always love and respect you."

"Thanks Baby Girl! Be sure to congratulate Porter and kiss the boys for me."

"I sure will Daddy. Bye for now."

"Bye." Uncle Clem smiled and said, "You Floods still know how to throw a grand shindig. The ceremony was amazing, and watching little Sterling walk his mama down the aisle was priceless."

140

"I couldn't agree more." He saw me giving the guests I couldn't recognize puzzled looks.

"All in due time son. You two need to get on back to your guests. Especially you, young lady. I'm sure that rooster of yours is back there waiting on his hen."

"Not more than his hen wanting to get back to her rooster."

"Well, I guess that's our cue. Enjoy yourselves. Bye for now."

"Bye all." We made it back upstairs, went in our cart and made a beeline back to the reception tent.

Watching them out there on the dance floor, holding each other tightly, staring into each other's eyes brought back so many good memories and made me wax nostalgic about Frankie.

Dinner, dancing and toasts carried us late into the evening, and before long, the guests said their goodbyes and began dispersing. Porter and CiCi are spending the night here and flying out to Hawaii tomorrow morning. So after a few more turns on the dance floor with my daughters and granddaughters, I called it a night and went to bed.

Less than an hour later, I heard screaming and a lot of commotion in the hallway outside of my room. When I made it to the staircase, everyone was standing outside CiCi and Porter's suite. When I made it to the doorway, Porter was lying on the floor. He was unresponsive, and Beverly was frantically applying CPR. I could hear sirens blaring outside, and what sounded like one of our helicopters. They loaded Porter onto the helicopter and took off for the hospital. CiCi was weeping uncontrollably and rocking back and forth in Bella's arms. I've never seen her like this, but I can definitely relate to how she must feel. Before they took off, she asked me if he was still tethered to his silver cord. It was impossible to tell, but a half an hour later, Beverly called and told me we'd lost Porter. He suffered a massive heart attack aboard the helicopter while en route to Druid City. Those were his people who came over with Uncle Clem. That's why I didn't recognize them. An occasion so beautiful can turn terribly tragic in the twinkling of an eye. Life is a very fickle mystery. It's like Grammy used to say, 'Life can kick you in the teeth one moment, then kiss you on the lips in the next.' But like any storm we've ever faced, we'll get through this one together too.

CHAPTER 33

It feels like Porter's passing has cast a huge pall over this family, especially here on the farm. It feels as if we're all caught in a fog, and hopelessly waiting for some sunlight to burn it away.

CiCi's doing her best to put on a brave front and act as if she's ok. But I believe I know better than anyone how she really feels. Losing a loved one is never easy, but it's doubly harder to bear when it's your spouse. I don't know if I'm more concerned about her or Sterling. He's nine and understands what it means to die. Porter was his hero, and it's tough for a boy to lose his father. I know the feeling all too well. P.J.'s only a toddler, so it'll be a little easier for him. But despite his young age, even he knows something's not right.

I'm trying to get CiCi to open up to me and express her true feelings. It's ok for her to mourn, scream, cry, or even talk to a therapist if it'll begin the process of mending her heart. I'm sure he'll visit her before long, and I'm positive he'll remind her about how important she was to him and is to the family. I know he wants her to be happy and care for their sons. He'll also tell her that should love ever knock on her heart's door again, it's ok with him if she answers and allows it in.

I'm spending every moment I possibly can with her. I see her eyes light up with excitement whenever any of our people pay us a visit. I also feel her sadness when Porter isn't one of them. His relatives have come to her and told her he's ok, but she wants to see and hear from him directly.

Aside from keeping close tabs on her, I feel better physically than I've felt in a long time. I suppose being needed can energize anyone. And the support our entire family and community have given her and those boys is truly gratifying. Watching my children and grandchildren look to her for leadership really makes my heart glad. It shows me how much they respect me and our family legacy. They understand the significance of it continuing without end.

A couple of weeks later, she was driving me back to the farm after my regular checkup at the clinic. When all of a sudden, she pulled over to the shoulder of the road, stopped the car, burst into tears and wept loudly.

144

I didn't say a word, I just took her hand in mine and let her get the pain out. Before long, she wiped her eyes, smiled and said, "Everything's going to be fine now, Gramps! Ever since Porter's passing, I've been praying to see and talk to him one last time. Last night, he came to me in a dream. He said he wanted to wait a while before coming. He said he didn't want to come the way everyone else did, he wanted to come directly through my heart. He thanked me for my love, our sons and for making him happier than he'd ever dreamed was possible. He told me to live, laugh, love and of course lead. He said should love ever find me again, don't hesitate to claim it because it's truly the greatest power in the universe. I know he was there because I slept really well for the first time since he's been gone. I understand Gramps, and to know you experienced it twice and kept moving forward has buoyed my faith as well."

"You just said a mouthful there, Baby Girl, and I'm thrilled to see you get up off the canvas, dust yourself off, lace up your gloves and fight through another storm. I'm so very proud of you, not just me but every single Flood-ancestor and descendant. Now start this car and get us home. If I'm not mistaken, we're having fried chicken tonight."

"Yes sir, right away." With a giggle and a twist of the ignition, we started for home.

Charles R. Butts Jr.

CHAPTER 34

Life's rhythm synced with ours once more. The sun rose and set, the moon and stars owned the night, and seasons continued to change. Those changes brought some significant surprises right along with them. For one, I wouldn't have bet on me still being around a year later. But I still am, and feeling well to boot. The second surprise has been CiCi finding love again so quickly. I've always believed that true, lasting love seeks and finds you. I believe when you seek love, it's never real and it never lasts.

While up in Atlanta visiting with one of her cousins, they met David for dinner at one of our steakhouses. David brought Michael, who serves as Atlanta's mayor. Long story short, from that night on, they've been inseparable.

Love has found them both, and seven months later they were engaged. I suggested she slow down long enough for him to understand her and her son's significance to our family.

We explained our history, and he said he definitely wants to be a husband to CiCi and a step-father to Sterling and P.J. We wanted him to be sure because he's a rising star in the political arena. He's even being pushed to run for Governor in the next general election. He assured me he has no political ambitions beyond that and would happily join the private sector after his term expires, should he even be elected.

They've decided to wait until New Year's Eve to get married. She wants to do it at David's estate in Atlanta. I can surely understand that. Her last wedding ceremony held at the farm didn't have a happy ending, and with Atlanta being a more neutral and an international city, I thought it would be perfect.

When the wedding day arrived, she surprised me by asking me to give her away. When I asked if she thought one of her uncles or cousins would be better, she smiled and said, "I've already asked the greatest man I've ever known to give me away. I insist."

"I'd be honored."

As we stood at the rear of one of the most beautiful churches my tired eyes have ever seen, we looked past the officiating minister and attendants. There were a lot of our kinfolks seated in the choir stand. When we reached the altar, Uncle Clem winked and nodded, where my parents, grandparents, great-great grandparents were all smiling and waving. After officially giving CiCi away, I took my seat and alternated watching the ceremony and our people.

After the reception, I sat on the veranda with Clement and David. We had a couple of drinks, a cigar and a lot of laughs. After that, and right before going into the house to go to bed, Uncle Clem showed up.

"Hey nephew!"

"Hey Unc, how's it going?"

"Great! That was a wonderful ceremony. We're in great hands, you should be proud. But if I'm not mistaken, I recall a young man doing the same thing more than half a century ago."

"I am proud Unc, not so much of myself, but of CiCi. I've never met a spirit like that one before. She was full of fire and intelligence. She doesn't allow anything to hold her down for long; leader, wife and mother. She wears all the hats very well. She's made my life so much easier."

"She does indeed. God definitely knew what He was doing. He knew exactly what we needed. You'll never admit it, but you played a huge part in her upbringing. She's who she is in part because of you and Frankie."

"I sleep extremely well at night Unc. Just knowing the heights this family's set up to reach and exceed."

"Amen to that. Well, I'm going to go on and let you get some rest. Goodnight."

"Goodnight Unc."

CHAPTER 35

I t's a couple of days away from Thanksgiving, and I admittedly have much to be thankful for. My health and strength are just the icing on life's cake. All is well with the family, we continue to flourish. Everyone's content and couldn't be better.

If I've learned one thing these past couple of years is nothing is certain and the journey is always unpredictable. I've also learned that dreading anything or waiting for the next shoe to drop will surely bring it to pass. We indeed are the sum total of our thoughts, whatever you think you create. From time to time, even I have to be reminded of this particular truth. Because of this, I count every moment and everything as a joyous one.

I love it when everyone comes back home. Spending time with my family is far more important than a date on the calendar. I'm grateful for the dates nonetheless, because they provide the occasion.

CiCi and Michael are quite the affectionate couple. They both are immensely in love and excited about their baby that's due in January. She's getting the little girl she's always wanted. Even though she loves her two sons to the moon and back, she's always wanted a daughter. Her pregnancy came as a surprise because she was previously told she could no longer have children. Since Michael doesn't have any of his own, he's just bursting with excitement. That little girl won't lack for love, that's for sure. And knowing our family tree has sprouted another branch pleases everyone.

Despite spending a lot of her time in Atlanta, she and I talk and spend time frequently. Here at home, I'm out and about more. On Thanksgiving Day, I even volunteered to help serve meals at the shelter.

After our family Thanksgiving supper, I decided to go down under the greenhouse for some whiskey and a cigar. Afterward, on my way back to the house, I slipped on the stairs and fell to the floor. I was in excruciating pain and there was no one there to help. Unable to get to the phone or intercom, I was forced to just lie there and pray that someone came looking for me. Fortunately, my grandson Winston and his son Kayden came along.

At the hospital, I learned my lower leg was fractured in two places. The cast covered my leg, to slightly above my knee. I also tore a ligament in my knee. It's definitely true that the older you get, the weaker your body becomes. I suppose donating all that marrow didn't help things either. The orthopedist thought it would be best for my fractures to heal before repairing my knee.

Before being discharged, a motorized chair was custom made for me. I was disappointed at the thought of being dependent on others for a while, but looking forward to rehabbing and getting back on my feet again. A determined Flood can never be held down for too long.

CHAPTER 36

Patience is a virtue that must be earned. There aren't any shortcuts to attaining it. Only those deemed worthy possess and understand it. After twelve weeks, the cast was removed, and I was given a walker. Six weeks after that, the ligament in my knee was repaired. Nearly three months later, I limped into rehab with my cane. I was ready to put in the work. I will go under the greenhouse again, I'll even use the stairs if I want.

Naturally, this ordeal scared the family and I was fussed over daily. Personally, I saw it as another challenge I was determined to overcome. Needless to say, I came away from all of this proud of myself and even stronger for having passed through another storm.

In the middle of February, little Frances Kathleen was born. I should have known she'd be named after Frankie and Kathy. I know in my heart, they're just as proud of the name as I am. Maybe the next one with sight will come through her.

While asleep the other night, Frankie came to me in a dream. She told me how much she misses me and how anxious she is about our reunion. I asked her when it would be, and she laughed and said it would be sooner rather than later. I woke up the next morning missing her even more.

With our annual Memorial Day picnic only a couple of days away, I find myself feeling a little strange. Overall, I'm in good health, but every now and then I'm overcome by an amazing rush of heat to the point of profuse sweating and slight dizziness. I haven't seen Uncle Clem in months and neither CiCi nor I can make head or tails of it. The only logical take on it is that my journey is nearing its conclusion. If that's the case, I'm more than ready. Truth be told, I'm positive. I've squeezed every ounce of happiness, joy and life out of this ride. More than my fair share, really. And with CiCi not showing a hint of fear or doubt, I know everything, and everyone will be just fine.

Unbeknownst to me, the cookout is a celebration of my life. It's my birthday, Christmas and Father's Day all rolled up into one. A bigger surprise was everyone moving back here. Even though they're doing it for me, I'm just so happy to have everyone here. They are definitely showing me the time of my life. There's nothing but an amazing outpouring of joy and love taking place. Besides that, there's no greater gift than sharing it with family and friends. It sure makes an old, lonely man a little less lonely.

CHAPTER 37

I find myself unable to explain how I'm feeling these days. Physically, I feel fine, and besides feeling an incredible rush of searing heat flow through me from time to time, I feel wonderful.

Not only am I'm aware that my time is drawing near, the entire family knows as well. Every day is full of fun and I appear to be the center of everyone's attention. I count it all joy though, just more opportunities to create and tuck away more memories in my heart.

What pleases me most is the incredible unity, strength and synergy of love we have for each other. Of all the things I was charged to do in Uncle Clem's stead, this is what's made me the proudest. And

I'm proud to say, I've seen more than my share of families blessed with even more than we have, to crumble even faster.

I just want to appreciate and be present in every moment I have remaining. I plan to savor every meal, cigar and drink of whiskey I consume. I want to continue to take in as much as the world's beauty that I can - every sunrise, sunset and everything in between.

I know I'm ready because I haven't seen Uncle Clem or any of our people from the other side in months. I'm still able to see spirits, just unable to see any of my people.

During the evenings after supper, CiCi and I sit outside and talk. I smoke and drink while we just watch life happen all around us. The wind blows, the sun rises, shines and sets and darkness of night appears in its absence. Beautiful sounds and smells of living and growing things, all assembled to function flawlessly in God's divine order.

One evening, while sitting on my favorite bench watching the moon and twinkling stars in silence, CiCi put her hand in mine and asked, "How are you feeling Gramps, is your time near?"

"I believe so, Baby Girl. I know I didn't even have to tell you because I know your heart already has. I can hardly wait to see your Grandma. I'm pretty sure this is my last night here, but I'm proud to know you'll be steering the ship in my stead. Never forget that we'll always be around whenever you need us."

"I'm not worried Gramps, nor do I feel any fear. I know everything's going to be just fine. You've taught me so much, but the greatest lesson has been that no storm lasts forever. Eventually, they pass through and the sun comes out again."

"That's exactly right. I'd like for you to be with me when my Frankie comes for me tomorrow. Will you?"

"Of course Gramps! I can't think of no higher honor. I believe it should always be that way. The successor seeing their predecessor off."

"Thanks Baby Girl, tomorrow's gonna be truly special."

"It'll indeed Gramps."

Charles R. Butts Jr.

CHAPTER 38

After a sound and refreshing night of sleep, I woke up feeling amazing. The moon was still out and apparently, I'm even up before the roosters. After a prayer, I showered and dressed before taking the elevator down to the main floor. With coffee in hand, I stepped outside and took a seat on my favorite bench that faces eastward. I have a feeling this is the very last sunrise I'm ever going to see. I don't want to miss a second of it.

Gratitude and love fill my heart now. As I now watch the dawning of a new day, I'm grateful to be in decent health and present in this beautiful moment. I can't help but reflect on my journey.

I've seen, laughed, lived, labored and loved every step of the way. Now it's time for me to pass over to be with my ancestors, my beloved Frankie and of course, my God.

It wasn't too long before I heard people stirring about and smelled breakfast cooking. CiCi came outside with her coffee and sat right beside me. "Good morning Gramps, how are you feeling today?"

"Good morning Baby Girl! I feel mighty fine, in fact I feel strong enough to take a long trip."

"Where?" she asked. When she thought about it for a second she continued, "Oh, I forgot, is today is the day?"

"I believe it is, Baby Girl." She put her arm around me, kissed me on the cheek and said, "Don't worry about a thing Gramps. I'm ok, and everyone will be just fine. We'll continue to march onward and upward while honoring our incredible legacy."

"That sure does make me feel good. You're an amazing leader who's going to do great things."

"I promise I will Gramps. And once my heart reveals the next one, I'll immediately begin preparing them to succeed me someday."

"I know, and my heart has already shown me. You have everything you need to lead them tucked away inside of that huge heart of yours."

"What do you want to do today, Gramps?"

"Any and everything I possibly can. I plan to soak in as much of this life as I can today. But, in order to do that, I suppose I need to eat a hearty breakfast. And to keep the mood light all day, I won't tell anyone else until supper. Deal?"

"It's a deal Gramps, whatever you say. Now let's go eat."

After breakfast, I went for a walk before going into town for a haircut and shave. Then we stopped by the parlor, so I could give CiCi the file containing my arrangements and my new modified will. It's a warm and sunny December day. A few puffy clouds dot an otherwise blue sky. We had lunch at the diner across the square before finally returning to the farm in the early afternoon.

Back at home in the parlor, I talked and laughed with all of my kids, grandkids and great-grandkids. I can sense they all know what's about to happen. I thought about it and changed my mind about telling them during supper. I also made CiCi promise to not say anything either.

After a lively supper, I had a cigar and a drink with all the menfolk. We reminisced and shared laughs, while they peppered me with questions about the days gone by. I eventually finished fellowshipping, and I met CiCi on our favorite bench in front of the cemetery. From this vantage point, we're able to see the setting sun. Hues of red, orange and gold mesh with the bluish sky, as the sun descends below the horizon. Only to be replaced by a full moon and constellations of bright stars blanketing the night sky.

"Isn't this beautiful, Baby Girl?"

"It sure is Gramps. It's something I'll never get tired of seeing."

"Me neither." CiCi took my hand in hers and said, "It's time, isn't it Gramps?"

"Just about, my ride is almost here." In that instant, I felt my body tensing up and I could hardly catch my breath. Dizzy, and overcome by an incredible rush of heat. I heard a slight pop and could see myself hovering above my body. When I turned back, I saw my head slumped on CiCi's shoulder. It all happened so fast, I could hardly believe it.

"So this is what it feels like!" I said to CiCi.

Smiling through the tears streaming down her eyes, she said, "You're free Gramps! How does it feel?"

"I feel so light and free Baby Girl, like I can fly. I'm like a butterfly emerging from its cocoon." We then saw a car roaring up the drive. It resembled the Porsche 911 Frankie drove when she picked me up from the airport all those years ago. She pulled up next to the bench, smiled, and asked, "Do you need a ride, old man?"

"Why yes ma'am, I surely do."

"Well hop in handsome. We have places to go, folks to see and things to do." Turning towards CiCi she said, "Hey Sweetie, thanks for taking such good care of him for me."

"The honor was all mine, Gram." I got in the car, closed the door and said, "Ok Baby Girl, It's officially your show now. Take the baton, lead well, and know we'll always be here for you."

"When will I see you again?"

"Soon, real soon." Frankie put the car in gear, and we zoomed down the drive a bit and faded out of sight. We rode right across the river into forever.

Charles R. Butts Jr.

CHAPTER 39

Three days later, when CiCi was down under the greenhouse recording my passing in the family bible, Uncle Clem and I showed up.

"Hey there, Baby Girl! It's me! I just wanted to thank you for such a wonderful home going. Be sure to tell everyone how much I love them and how proud I was to see such an amazing outpouring of love."

"Wow Gramps! Pictures definitely didn't do you any justice. I can definitely see why Gram loves you so." Uncle Clem laughed and I blushed.

"Thanks Baby Girl, I just wanted to thank you for everything I've witnessed these past three days." Uncle Clem smiled, then said "We're not surprised though, none of us are. You're going to do great things for the family. Never forget to listen and follow your heart. It will never lead you wrong."

"We'll always be here for you too, always and forever."

"Thanks Gramps, thanks Unc, that's always comforting to know, and I'll never tire of hearing that."

"Always welcome," we said in unison.

"Speaking of tiring, looks like it won't be long before our family tree sprouts another branch. I imagine it'll be harder for you to get around in a few months. Congratulations!"

CiCi's eyes lit up and she asked," How did you know? Oh, never mind. I'm going to the clinic today for a test to confirm what the three of us already know. I haven't even told Michael yet."

"I'm sure he's going to be very happy."

"Yes, I know he will be. What's it like over there Gramps? Can you describe it for me?"

"It's beyond description; try to imagine the beauty, perfection of the greatest sunrise and sunset you've ever seen. Now magnify that by infinity. And this is just what I've witnessed so far. I've yet to experience the beauty and grandeur of heaven in its totality. Truth be told, most of us here haven't even begun to scratch its surface."

"Wow, I'll just have to see it when I see it. I'm in no hurry though; I have a critical job to do here. This is where my focus is."

"Well said! We're going to leave now, I've got to get back to your Grandmother. You know how fussy she can be."

"You go Gramps! See you later Big Unc!"

"Bye now."

Charles R. Butts Jr.

CHAPTER 40

Generation after generation, the Floods will continue to prosper. Each passing and every birth will leave and create an indelible mark on our incredible legacy. The earth will continue to revolve around the sun and time will keep moving forward. Life will continue to grow and expand and I'm prayerful that any future risks taken will continue to be rewarded by faith. The strength of our family's bond will forever be tied by ropes of faith, hope and love…. and more importantly, our rich bloodline. They'll face and conquer the storms to come without getting stuck in them. The storms will pass, and our tree will continue to grow and thrive!

Charles R. Butts Jr.

TO PUBLISH YOUR
STORY OR BOOK

CONTACT

WILLIAMS & KING PUBLISHERS
888-645-0550
Info@WilliamsAndKingPublishers.com

OR

TO LEARN ABOUT
OTHER BOOKS
PUBLISHED BY

WILLIAMS & KING PUBLISHERS

VISIT

WilliamsAndKingPublishers.com

www.ingramcontent.com/pod-product-compliance
Lightning Source LLC
Chambersburg PA
CBHW070030260626
47159CB00005B/2002